He had to get to her. Had to warn her.

As he struggled to get up, his head spun and he collapsed on the pavement. He coached himself to breathe, to think past the throbbing headache long enough to help Jenna.

An innocent woman protecting an innocent child.

"Matthew?"

He looked up. Colorful green eyes sparkled down at him. Jenna.

No, they'd find her; they'd kill her. "You need to..."

What? Be taken into FBI custody? Why? He was in no shape to protect her, and by the time backup arrived, the thugs would have surely found her.

"My keys." He dug into his jacket pocket and fished them out. As he offered them to her, they slipped through his trembling fingers. "Take the truck. Get out of here."

He heard the keys scrape against the pavement. Good. She was taking his advice. Looking out for herself and the child.

A few seconds passed, maybe minutes; he couldn't be sure. What he did know was that if the cops found him they'd ask questions, risking his cover.

Then again, he could tell the truth, to a point. He'd been jumped and beaten, and when he regained consciousness his truck was gone.

"Open your eyes."

It was Jenna's voice.

He blinked a few times and found himself looking up at her beautiful face.

An eternal optimist, **Hope White** was born and raised in the Midwest. She and her college sweetheart have been married for thirty years and are blessed with two wonderful sons, two feisty cats and a bossy border collie. When not dreaming up inspirational tales, Hope enjoys hiking, sipping tea with friends and going to the movies. She loves to hear from readers, who can contact her at hopewhiteauthor@gmail.com.

Books by Hope White

Love Inspired Suspense

Hidden in Shadows
Witness on the Run
Christmas Haven
Small Town Protector
Safe Harbor
Baby on the Run

Echo Mountain

Mountain Rescue
Covert Christmas
Payback
Christmas Undercover
Witness Pursuit
Mountain Ambush

Visit the Author Profile page at Harlequin.com.

Baby on the Run

Hope White

Recycling programs
for this product may
not exist in your area.

® LOVE INSPIRED BOOKS

ISBN-13: 978-1-335-54356-1

Baby on the Run

This edition published by arrangement with Love Inspired Books.

www.Harlequin.com

Printed in U.S.A.

Be careful for nothing; but in every thing by prayer
and supplication with thanksgiving let your requests
be made known unto God.

—*Philippians* 4:6

Many thanks to expert moms
Stephanie Christanson and Cassy Patterson,
along with Deputy Sheriff Ryan Sherman
and FBI special agent Mike Johnson,
for their patience in answering my many questions.

ONE

"You need to protect little Eli."

Jenna North studied her friend. "What's this about, Chloe?"

Chloe gazed at her eighteen-month-old son as he clutched a small white polar bear in one hand and ran a wooden train across a coffee table with the other.

Paperwork had kept Jenna late at the Broadlake Foundation, where she worked as development manager, when she received Chloe's frantic call. Jenna offered to stop by Chloe's house on the way home, but Chloe rejected the idea. Instead, she came straight over to the school-turned-community-center where the foundation leased space. Jenna hadn't expected Chloe to bring Eli with her, not at this hour.

"I've made some bad choices," Chloe suddenly confessed.

Haven't we all? Jenna thought. "God forgives,

remember?" The words tasted bitter rolling off her tongue. "Chloe, what's going on?"

The young mother shook her head.

"Come on. I can't help unless—"

"I'm scared!"

Eli looked up at his mom with rounded eyes. She pulled him into her arms and rocked slightly. "I'm sorry, sweetie. I'm sorry." She eyed Jenna. "Promise me you'll protect him."

A chill ran down Jenna's spine. Could she truly make that promise considering she'd been unable to protect her own son?

And even herself?

"Please," Chloe begged.

Jenna nodded. "I promise."

Chloe sat back down, clinging to her son. Eli had other ideas. He squirmed against her, so Chloe put him down and he squatted to dig for another toy in his diaper bag. He pulled out a second train and waddled back to the coffee table. Tears formed in Chloe's eyes as she watched him.

Frustrated, Jenna wondered whom to call for help. Perhaps Chloe's counselor? Chloe had admitted to struggling with depression in the past.

"Have you called Rosalie?" Jenna asked.

"Why, you think I'm crazy?" Chloe snapped.

"No, I'm just not sure how to help you."

"You already have."

"Are you sure there isn't someone else?"

"Yes."

A few moments of silence passed between them.

"As long as he has Bubba, his bear, he'll be fine." Chloe handed Jenna a piece of paper. "If anything happens to me, keep Eli safe and find this man."

Jenna glanced at the note and slipped it into her pocket. "Who is it?"

"My cousin Marcus Garcia. He lives north of Missoula, in the mountains. Don't trust anyone else with Eli, okay?"

Jenna nodded. That wouldn't be a problem since trusting people was a skill she'd lost years ago.

"Marcus is the only family I've got," Chloe said, wistful.

"What about Gary?"

Chloe sighed. "I was so naive when I married him. I thought he was my Prince Charming."

Jenna knew that princes only existed in fairy tales.

"But he *is* Eli's father," Jenna said.

"Gary is a selfish man," Chloe said in a firm tone. "He doesn't care about us."

"Chloe—"

"He's dangerous." She pinned Jenna with intense eyes. "Gary is a monster."

Prickles skittered across Jenna's nerve endings. *Keep it together, Jenna.*

"Dangerous how?" Jenna pressed.

Chloe stood suddenly. "I'm going to be sick. Watch Eli." She rushed across the office and disappeared into the hallway.

"Chloe!" Jenna wanted to go after her, but couldn't leave Eli alone.

"Mama?" he said.

"She'll be right back, buddy."

He clung tighter to his bear. Jenna kneeled beside the table and struggled to smile at Eli. Her own son would have been a little older than Eli now.

I'm sorry, baby Joey.

"Stop," she whispered and turned her attention to the toddler. "Choo-choo, choo-choo," she said, running a small wooden train across the table. Eli grabbed another train and mimicked her action.

As she watched him intently move his train back and forth, she couldn't help but smile. There was something so pure about a child. Most of the time, when she was around kids, she was able to revel in that innocence instead of being pulled down by sadness. Sometimes it allowed a slight ray of hope to pierce through the darkness of her own grief, grief that drove her to start a new life in Cedar River, Montana.

The sound of shattering glass echoed down the hall. Jenna sat straight up.

"Let me go!" Chloe's voice echoed.

Jenna automatically rushed across the room

and snatched the canister of pepper spray out of her bag. She peeked into the hallway…

Two men were escorting Chloe to the exit: an unusually tall man wearing a knit ski cap, and a husky, broad-shouldered guy in a leather jacket.

Heart pounding, Jenna pulled out her phone to call for help. Her petite stature was no match for two thugs, even with her self-defense training and the pepper spray clutched in her hand.

"I won't let you hurt him!" Chloe shouted.

As Jenna's trembling finger pressed the 9-1-1 buttons, a male voice said, "What's going on?"

She peeked around the corner and spotted Police Chief Billings.

For once she was relieved the cops had arrived.

"Stop it!" Chloe squirmed against the tall man's grip.

"Release her," the chief said.

Jenna was about to announce her presence when the chief grabbed Chloe, spun her around and put her in a choke hold.

Paralyzed with fear, Jenna watched as Chloe struggled against his firm grip, kicking and thrashing.

The thrashing slowed.

Chloe's body went limp.

She fell to the ground.

Jenna darted out of sight. The floor seemed to tip sideways beneath her feet.

"Put her in the trunk," Chief Billings said.

No, this can't be happening. *Please, God, help me.*

He'd never listened before. Why should He start now?

"And find her son," he said.

"You think he's here?" one of the men asked.

"It's worth checking. Go room by room," he ordered.

Jenna's mind struggled to come up with an explanation for what she'd just witnessed, but there was none. Her fight-or-flight response kicked in. *Use it to your advantage*, she'd been taught after leaving Anthony three years ago.

Doors opened and closed down the hall. She had seconds to figure this out.

She softly locked her office door. Adrenaline rushing through her body, she considered her options. If only she could make it to the north lot where she'd parked her car.

Eli waved a wooden train. "Choo-choo!"

She snapped her attention to the little boy. As the men got closer, they'd surely hear the child's enthusiastic voice. She dashed through the adjoining closet into the classroom next door and yanked the fire alarm. The sharp squealing sound pierced through the air. She rushed back to her office and quickly but gently tucked Eli into his snowsuit. The wail of the alarm drowned out his wails of confusion and fear.

Focus. It's all about focus.

Is this why Chloe chose Jenna to protect Eli, because she sensed Jenna's dark past, her determination never to be a victim again? The word *victim* sent a surge of panic through her body.

Stay calm, she coached herself.

She couldn't wait for the fire department. She'd be dead before they got here.

You need to protect Eli.

She set the toddler down and put on her jacket, tucking the pepper spray in her pocket for easy access. Eli stumbled a few feet away, arms flailing, trying to get away from the shrill alarm.

Across the room, the doorknob twisted right and left.

In an almost disassociated state, Jenna unlocked her desk drawer, removed the false bottom and grabbed her stash of emergency money.

One at home, one at work. *Be ready for anything.*

Money tucked safely into her pocket, she shouldered the diaper bag, picked up Eli and handed him the polar bear. Clutching the bear, he continued to cry, so she unclipped a pacifier from a strap on the diaper bag and offered it to the little boy. He took it and instantly quieted, his eyes rounding like saucers.

Flinging her messenger bag over her other shoulder, she headed again for the storage room. Since the building had once been a school, it had connecting classrooms that would give her access to the north exit, closer to her car.

As she passed through the storage room, she noticed a few car seats they used when taking children on field trips in the van. She grabbed one and forged ahead.

She was a woman on a mission, a warrior who was not going to lose this battle. Not this time.

The wail of sirens echoed from outside. Good. That should chase the intruders away. Violent men connected to local law enforcement—not a surprise to Jenna.

She finally made it to the north end of the school. This was it. She actually might get away safely.

There was no *might* about it. She'd made a promise to protect Chloe's child.

Jenna would not fail.

Clinging to Eli, she pushed open the door to the outside. Floodlights designed to discourage trespassers lit the playground all the way to the secondary parking lot. A strong gust of wind slapped her cheeks as she headed for her car.

What if the men were right behind her?

Traumatic flashbacks replayed in her mind like a video on accelerated speed. She quickened her pace, as if running could get her away from the images.

He can't hurt you if he can't find you.

She approached the corner of the building.

Only a few hundred feet from the parking lot.

Her car.

Freedom.

Matt Weller had been on a break, eating a sandwich in the custodian's office and listening to the hockey game on the radio, when he'd heard a woman scream. He thought he'd imagined it at first and checked the closed-circuit video feed. Two men were dragging Mrs. McFadden to the exit. Just as Matt got up to help her, Chief Billings entered the building.

And strangled Mrs. McFadden.

Matt's first reaction was to get his weapon.

As he sprinted across the playground, the fire alarm rang from the building. Why would the perps lure the fire department to the scene? That made no sense whatsoever.

He approached the truck and considered his next move. They would have surely taken Mrs. McFadden's body away by now, removing the evidence.

But Matt knew there had been more than one woman in the building tonight. The lovely Jenna North had been at the center working late, as she often did.

The building was so peaceful when she was there, one of the reasons he liked the night shift.

Until tonight.

Matt climbed into the front seat and took a

calming breath. He needed to be smart about this, needed to protect his cover and Miss North at the same time.

Something caught his eye across the lot—Jenna North carrying a child and a car seat. Hang on—he knew she wasn't married and didn't have kids.

Then Matt saw them—the two perps heading straight for her on the other side of the building.

The woman was going to get herself killed.

Matt shoved his truck into gear and drove slowly toward the building where the innocent Miss North was about to walk straight into trouble.

He couldn't let that happen, no matter the risk.

As Jenna approached the corner of the building, Matt sped up. All it would take was an effective block. Yes, he'd innocently pull up between her and the men and play out his role of night janitor by warning them to leave the premises due to the fire alarm.

He stopped the truck, got out and motioned for Jenna to get down.

Instead, she whipped out a canister of pepper spray.

Matt put out one hand in surrender and pointed around the corner with his other hand.

Her green eyes widened.

He motioned for her to stay low, and then went around the back of his truck to confront the men.

But there was only one guy. Not good. Where was the other perp?

"Get away from the building!" Matt shouted. He had to play his part, although his navy blue custodian's uniform should make it clear who he was.

"My wife is in there!" the guy, midforties, wearing a knit ski cap, shouted.

Yeah, his wife.

"Have to wait for the all clear from the fire department!" Matt shouted.

The man nodded and turned away. Good, an easy fix.

Then Knit Cap Guy snapped around and took a swing at Matt. He dodged the blow and slugged the man in the stomach. He doubled over, coughing. With fisted hands, Matt readied himself for another assault.

The wail of sirens grew louder. The perp jumped to his feet and took off. Matt the FBI agent would chase after him; Matt the janitor would not.

He went back to the other side of the truck to help Jenna.

But she was gone.

He scanned the playground, the surrounding woods, the nearby parking lot. Knit Cap Guy's partner couldn't have gotten to her in the thirty seconds that Matt had been engaged in a fistfight.

Matt needed to find her, protect her.

He climbed into his truck to get his weapon and slammed the door.

A squeak echoed from the back seat.

He froze as he reached for the glove box and spun around. The little boy was sucking on a pacifier, eyes wide and curious, clutching a white stuffed animal.

"Are they gone?" Jenna said from the seat directly behind Matt.

He glanced in the rearview mirror. It seemed like her eyes had grown a brighter shade of green since he'd seen her earlier this evening.

"I think so," he said. "The little boy, is he Mrs. McFadden's?"

"Yes. I promised to protect him."

She studied Matt as if trying to make out his character, figure out whether he was good or bad. A little of both, he mused.

She needed good right now, very good, and committed. Which wasn't Matt. He wished it could be different. There was something about Jenna North that always made him smile. It was her way with staff members—with everyone, come to think of it. She was gentle and kind, yet persuasive enough to get the job done. The Broadlake Foundation thrived in part because of her fund-raising efforts that supported the operating budget.

He hoped she knew nothing about the cartel's

money-laundering scheme, that she was only an innocent bystander.

"My friend, Mrs. McFadden, she..." Jenna's voice trailed off.

He waited.

"She's dead."

Yes, Matt knew because he'd seen it happen.

And now, because she'd also witnessed the homicide, Miss North's life was in danger, as was the child's. Anger simmered in his chest. This couldn't be his problem, not today. He'd get Miss North and the child to safety and get back to his assignment.

Acting like the innocent bystander she assumed he was, Matt said, "We should report this."

"To whom? The police? They're involved."

"Why do you think that?"

"Chief Billings killed Chloe."

Great, not only had she been asked to protect the child, but she knew of the chief's involvement. This put her life at an even higher risk.

"Matthew, may I ask a favor?"

"Sure."

"Can you keep this between us, that you helped me, that I have Eli?"

"Only if you'll do me a favor in return."

"What?"

He had no choice but to protect her. She was in too deep. "Stay here until I deal with the fire department. Once they're gone, I'll come back and give you a ride to wherever you want to go. Okay?"

"Thank you, but my car isn't far."

"They'll probably be watching your car, right?"

She nibbled her lower lip for a second, an adorable gesture. He snapped his attention out the front window of his truck to the parking lot in the distance.

"I guess you're right," she said. "But…you should know that helping me could get you into trouble."

"I'm okay with that." Matt offered her the truck keys. "If I'm not back in twenty, take off."

He flung open the door and headed for the front of the building. He half expected to encounter the two perps, maybe even the chief, but they were nowhere in sight.

The glass windows on one of the community center doors had been shattered, which must be how the men had gained access to the building.

Motioning to the fire response crew, Matt led them inside. They spread out, looking for smoke. A fireman turned off the alarm and nodded at Matt. "Are you the night custodian?"

"Yes, sir."

"Please wait outside until we clear the building."

Matt did as he was ordered and called the police. He had to. It would look suspicious if he didn't alert the authorities to the break-in. As he was making the call, a squad car and the chief's car pulled into the lot.

A patrolman Matt recognized as Kyle Armstrong exited his squad car. Chief Billings and Kyle approached Matt.

You're only the janitor, he reminded himself.

"I was just calling you guys," Matt said.

"Hey, Matt," Kyle greeted him.

"You two know each other?" Billings asked.

"We attend the same church," Kyle said by way of explanation.

Church was no doubt a foreign concept to a guy like Billings. A dirty cop. A killer.

"This is Matt Weller, the night custodian," Kyle introduced.

Billings extended his hand. "Nice to meet you, Matt. Have any idea who pulled the alarm?"

"No, sir. Apparently some guy broke in." He pointed toward the broken window.

"Some guy? Not mischievous teens?" Billings asked.

Matt opted for sticking to the truth as much as possible. "No, it was a man, sir." He looked directly at Billings, whose eye twitched ever so slightly.

"Can you describe him?" Kyle asked, pulling out a small notebook.

"About five-ten, a hundred and eighty pounds." He directed the rest of his answer to Kyle. "He wore a black leather jacket and knit cap. I'm thinking he was pushing forty?"

"Wow, how close did you get to this guy?" Kyle asked.

"Pretty close. He took a swing at me."

"Are you injured?" Billings said with mock concern.

"No, sir. I grew up the youngest of five boys so I'm pretty good at defending myself."

"The knit cap perp was inside the building?" Kyle pushed.

"Actually we got into it outside, back by the playground."

Kyle looked up in question.

"I went out to my truck to get something, and that's when I encountered the man," Matt said. "The alarm had gone off—not sure what that was about. He claimed his wife was in the building."

"His wife?" Kyle said. "But the center was closed."

"That is correct," Matt said. "I thought I convinced him to leave, but then he went all Rocky on me."

The fire crew exited the building. "It's clear," the shift captain said.

"Thanks." Billings turned to Matt. "I'd like you to walk me through what happened tonight. Step by step."

Of course he did. He wanted to figure out if

Matt was telling the truth or creating a story to protect himself, Jenna and the little boy.

"Sure, this way." He led Kyle and the chief into the community center. By the end of this story, they'd be at Matt's truck. He hoped they wouldn't decide to search it, but why would they? Matt wasn't a suspect. If Jenna stayed down and the little boy didn't cry, Billings wouldn't find her.

She'd be hiding right under his nose.

"I was in the back office on break, listening to the hockey game," Matt said.

They got to his office and the cops poked their heads inside.

"Closed circuit?" Kyle asked, eyeing the monitor.

"Yep. For security." Matt curled his fingers into his palm to keep calm. "It gives me a view of the main hallway."

"You didn't see the suspect break in?"

"No, he probably accessed the building while I was at my truck." He feigned panic and looked at Kyle. "Man, I hope I don't lose my job over this—I mean for not preventing the break-in."

"If he was determined to get in, nothing would have stopped him," Billings said.

Matt nodded. Was that subtext? A subtle warning?

"Continue," Chief Billings said.

"So about ten thirty I went out to the truck." He led them to the back door and swung it open. The three men ambled outside. "It wasn't parked this close originally, but kids were finishing up basketball when I arrived at six. I figured as long as I was out here I'd repark closer to the building."

"Besides the basketball league, who else was here tonight, Mr. Weller?" the chief asked.

"A yoga class, line dancing for seniors and the knitting club. They were all gone by nine."

"Anyone else, perhaps employees working late?" Billings pushed.

Matt wondered if he'd seen Jenna North's little blue car parked in the overflow lot. He had to play this just right, be as truthful as possible.

"I might have seen Jenna North earlier. She works for a foundation that leases space here."

"I'll look into it," Kyle said.

Chief Billings eyed Matt speculatively, and he broke eye contact in his effort to act submissive and nonthreatening.

Innocent.

That's when Matt noticed the back window of his truck was cracked open. Matt needed a quick redirect to get them away from Jenna and the child.

"We got into a fistfight over here." Matt led them to the other side of the truck. "Actually, there was one other thing about the knit cap guy."

Billings's eyes flared.

"He had a scar above his eyebrow here." Matt pointed to his own forehead.

"That could help," Kyle said.

"I yelled at him to stay away from the building. He yelled back that his wife was inside, which made no sense. Then he threw a punch. That's about it."

"That's a lot," Kyle said, jotting notes furiously.

The chief kneeled, analyzing something on the ground.

"What is it, sir?" Kyle asked.

"Found a cigarette butt. I'll bag it."

Except Knit Cap Guy hadn't been smoking, which meant Billings was trying to throw the investigation off course.

"Can you tell us anything else, Matt?" Kyle said.

"No, sorry. I'd better go fix the front door, and I should probably call Mrs. Harris, my boss."

"If anything else does come to mind, please call me directly." Billings handed him a business card.

"Will do. Thanks."

Matt led the cops back to the front of the building, and the knot in his gut uncoiled as they got farther away from the truck, from Jenna and the little boy.

He called Lucinda Harris and explained the situation as he watched the fire trucks pull away. She was worried about Matt and told him to finish cleaning up the mess and leave early. A good thing, since he was desperate to check on Jenna and the child.

The chief and Kyle were still out front, assessing and speculating.

Matt went inside and found a piece of wood from the storage area to cover the broken window. He secured it in place and swept up the mess. He wanted to play the role of night custodian a little longer, until the cops left the premises.

And then he needed to get to Jenna and the child. Let her know everything was okay.

He started flipping off main lights. Through one of the community room windows, he noticed the two police cars pulling out of the lot.

After jogging to the back of the building, he got his jacket out of the office, locked the building and headed to his truck. He grabbed the door handle, but it was locked. Fearful of being found, Miss North must have locked the doors. He tapped twice, blowing on his chilled hands, and glanced over his shoulder out of habit.

The door unlocked with a click. He climbed into the front seat. "They're gone."

He felt the barrel of a gun pressed against the back of his head.

TWO

Jenna's hand trembled as she aimed the gun at the janitor's head. Of course there was no way she could pull the trigger, but she didn't know what else to do.

I might have seen Jenna North earlier, he'd said to the chief.

The man who'd killed her best friend.

Matthew might as well have opened the truck door and handed Jenna and Eli over to the guy.

"I know you're scared—"

"Drive," she interrupted.

"Please put the gun down."

"Now." She tapped the barrel against his head, not hard, but hard enough.

With a nod, he started the truck and pulled out of the lot.

She still couldn't believe what she'd found when she'd gone through his glove box looking for a tissue.

Zip ties, duct tape and a gun.

Who was this man? Had she run from one killer directly into the arms of another?

The trembling intensified, running down her arm to rock her entire body. No, she would not let the trauma of the past consume her; she would not fall apart.

This time she'd save the child.

She had considered fleeing in his truck, but that would have meant driving past the killer police chief.

"I can explain," Matthew said.

"Just drive."

"To where?"

Good question. The mall was closed at this time of night, yet she needed a very public place to regroup. And then what?

One step at a time.

"I-90 truck stop." It was very public and not far away. She wouldn't spend a minute longer than necessary with this creep. Once away from the janitor, she'd call someone for help. But whom? Patrice, the woman who'd helped Jenna escape Anthony?

Wait—she remembered the slip of paper Chloe had given her with the name of her cousin. That's it. She'd call Marcus to come get her.

"I don't know what you're thinking, Miss North, but if I'd wanted to do you harm I would have turned you over to Chief Billings."

"Then you wouldn't have the pleasure of hurting me."

He shot her an intense look through the rear-view mirror. "I would never hurt you. I want to help."

"Stop talking," she ordered as the past taunted her.

I want to help you get better.

She'd believed her abusive husband. Only after she'd left Anthony did she understand how his words had been an insidious and powerful manipulation.

"At least let me call someone for you," Matthew said.

You need help.

She almost told the janitor to shut up again, but decided to speak the truth instead. "Stop pretending to be my friend. I heard you tell Billings that I was at the center tonight."

"I had to. Your car was a hundred yards away."

Her car. She'd never get it back. They'd impound it, making it harder for her to flee the city.

Which meant she'd have to rely on strangers for help until Chloe's cousin could rescue her.

No, you don't need rescuing any longer.

The janitor turned left.

"Where are you going? I said take me to the truck stop." Fear skittered across her shoulders. Was he going to try to overpower her? In front of Eli?

"We're being followed," he said.

She snapped her gaze out the back window. Headlights shone through the dark night. "That could be anyone."

"They've been behind us since we left the center."

"Just get me to the truck stop."

"Yes, ma'am."

As he drove through town, she scolded herself for trusting him in the first place, but Matthew had seemed like an innocuous sort of man. She'd heard he'd moved to town after serving in the military and that he'd even joined the local church. That in and of itself would have made most people trust him.

Yet Anthony had been a church leader, a pillar of the community—and behind closed doors, he was a monster.

Like Chloe's husband?

Like the man driving the truck?

Why did Jenna attract violent men? Maybe her stepfather had been right when he'd branded her a stupid and weak girl, a lost cause.

"No," she ground out.

"Ma'am?"

She snapped her attention to him. "What?"

"You said something?"

She clenched her jaw. This was not the time for the past to taunt her. Making bad choices when it came to romance seemed to be a habit for Jenna, starting with Mike in high school, and then Anthony. It had taken two years and a miscarriage to get away from her abuser. Tonight, three years after her escape, she found herself right back in the eye of the storm.

This time she'd get it right. She'd protect her friend's little boy.

Her friend. Chloe.

The image of Chloe collapsing on the floor flashed across Jenna's mind. Still in shock about the loss, Jenna had had no time to process or grieve. Chloe wouldn't want her to be distracted; she'd want Jenna to put all her energy into saving Eli.

Chloe was a young mother who'd become Jenna's best friend in town after they'd met on the development committee for the foundation. They'd joined an exercise dance class and regularly gone out for pie afterward. They had the same sense of humor, the same view on life.

It seemed they had other similarities as well—their bad choices in men.

The janitor made a right turn, heading in the opposite direction of her requested destination.

"Hey." She tapped the barrel of the gun against his head.

"Look, trust me or don't trust me. I don't care," he said. "At least let me lose the tail before I drop you at the truck stop."

"You can drop the knight-in-shining-armor act. I'm not buying it."

"Then shoot me."

She snapped her gaze to the rearview mirror. He pinned her with fierce blue eyes.

"Shoot me or let me lose them. Your choice," he said.

She glanced nervously at Eli. She couldn't pull the trigger with a baby in the car.

Who was she kidding? She couldn't pull the trigger, period.

But this creep didn't have to know that.

"Fine, lose them," she said.

"Yes, ma'am."

He sped up, and she jerked back in her seat. She glanced beside her at Eli. The motion hadn't disturbed him from his restful slumber as he sucked on his Binky and clung to his bear.

The janitor navigated down side streets and back up an alley. She clutched the gun grip to stay grounded, but wished it were something else, something spiritual. Her fingers automatically went to the base of her neck, remembering the dove charm she'd worn as a child, a charm that symbolized the Holy Spirit.

A charm she'd ripped off and thrown away as a teenager after she'd lost faith in an absent god.

She thumbed the silver ring on her right hand instead, the braided knot given to her by Patrice, who'd taken Jenna in and helped her heal after she'd left Anthony. The interwoven strands of silver represented connectedness, a reminder that Jenna was never alone, that she could always call on Patrice and the guardian network for support.

Matthew pulled onto the expressway. They were leaving town and heading in the right direction.

"We're good," he said.

"Hardly," she muttered.

"Listen—"

"Don't speak!" she said, louder than she'd intended.

Eli's eyes popped open and he started to cry. "Shh, I'm sorry, little one," she said, fearing she was the wrong person to be caring for a child.

To appease him, she sang a song, one her mom had sung to her when she was little. The little boy's eyes widened with curiosity, and then his eyelids blinked slowly and finally closed.

The car grew eerily silent as they left town and continued on the expressway. She liked the silence, embraced it. It gave her time to think.

About fifteen minutes later, the janitor exited the expressway, pulled into the truck stop and parked.

She removed the gun magazine and pocketed it, opened the truck door and hurled the gun into the snow-covered field bordering the lot. Shouldering the diaper and messenger bags, she unbuckled the car seat.

"You sure you'll be okay?" he said.

She ignored his mock concern and lifted baby Eli out of the car. The little boy still clung to his bear for comfort.

Whether Chloe's cousin came to pick her up or Jenna called a taxi, she'd need the car seat for Eli. She grabbed it with her other hand.

"For what it's worth, I'm a cop," he said.

She froze and glared at the back of his head.

"Not local," he continued as if he anticipated her fear. "I'm undercover FBI."

"Sure you are." She shouldered the door shut and marched away from the truck. Did he think her that gullible?

Thick, wet snowflakes swirled around her as she crossed the parking lot. There were a dozen trucks and cars in the lot. Good, the more people around the safer she'd feel.

Once inside, she placed the car scat by the door. She considered what to do with the magazine of bullets. Maybe she should have kept the weapon to defend herself and Eli. She'd learned how to use a firearm after she'd escaped Anthony.

No, the thought of shooting someone made her nauseous, and it didn't feel right disposing of the magazine in a public place where it could end up in the wrong hands.

Instead, she decided to ditch her cell in case they could track it, and tossed the phone into the garbage can. She carried Eli to a nearby pay phone and called Chloe's cousin, but it went to voice mail.

"You've reached Marcus. I'm not here. Leave a message."

"Hi, Marcus. You don't know me, but I'm Jenna, a good friend of your cousin Chloe's. She told me to call you. There's been an emergency and I need your help. It's about Chloe's son, Eli. Anyway, I'm calling from a pay phone, but I'm not sure how long we'll be here. I guess I'll keep calling. Thanks."

What a message to leave a stranger. Would he even take her seriously?

She couldn't worry about that now.

As she headed into the twenty-four-hour store, a list of what to do next formed in her mind. First, she had to change her appearance. She bought a local football team knit ski cap to cover her dark hair. She'd tuck it up into the cap until she got the chance to color it.

After making her purchases, she would take her contacts out and replace them with her thick-rimmed glasses to further mask her identity. But what about Eli? Her gaze drifted to a pink child's ski cap. Disguising him as a girl would certainly throw someone off at first glance. She bought some cheap makeup, something she rarely wore, and scissors for cutting her hair. She wished they had hair dye, but that would have to wait until she found a drugstore.

Her panic about not being able to protect Eli was subsiding. She'd made it safely away from the office, away from a corrupt killer cop.

She was proud of herself for getting this far.

Thanks to Matthew the janitor.

"A guy with zip ties, duct tape and a gun in his glove box," she muttered.

I'm undercover FBI.

She briefly wondered if he was being honest and her trauma had blinded her to the truth. No, why would an FBI agent keep duct tape in his car? He'd tried to explain, but she hadn't let him.

Peeking out the store window, she spotted Matthew talking on the phone as he picked up his weapon from the snow-covered field.

Movement suddenly drew her attention left.

The two men from the community center got out of a black car. She gasped and ducked behind a display of snacks, clutching Eli securely against her chest.

What if they came into the truck stop and saw the car seat by the door?

Seconds stretched like hours.

Stop hiding like a coward!

With a fortifying breath, she went back to the counter and peeked out the window.

The cashier stepped up and blocked her view. "May I help you?"

Jenna glanced around her into the parking lot.

The twentysomething cashier with long blond hair also glanced outside. Just as…

The two thugs from the community center jumped Matthew.

"Whoa," the girl said.

"I need to use your phone."

"There's a pay phone—"

"I'll give you twenty bucks."

Matt couldn't leave Jenna North at the truck stop without knowing she'd be okay.

He called in to give his boss an update. "She's a part of it now."

"You don't know that," his supervisor, Steve Pragge, said.

"Billings is after her."

There was a pause, then, "Not our problem. You need to get back to town and be ready for your shift tomorrow."

"And leave an innocent woman and child at the mercy of a killer?"

"If you're that worried, I'll send someone to bring her in."

"I doubt she'll go willingly."

"Then you bring her in. As long as you're back at work tomorrow night."

"I'm not sure she'll come with me either."

"What's the problem?"

"She doesn't trust cops."

"I don't know what you want me to say here,

Weller. This woman is a complication. You've got a job to do."

His boss ended the call, and Matt considered the subtext to Pragge's words. He expected Matt to stay on task, return to Cedar River and leave Jenna behind.

Not happening.

Matt wondered what had made Jenna do the about-face from trusting Matt to being terrified of him. The way she'd threatened him with the gun…

The gun. She'd retrieved it from his glove box. Since she probably had little if any experience with firearms, he could only guess what conclusions she would have drawn about someone who casually carried a handgun in his vehicle.

He went into the field to search for his gun and realized he wasn't angry that she'd tossed it. In fact, he respected her for the move if she thought him dangerous.

Scanning the area with a flashlight, he wondered how to convince Jenna to accept his help. He couldn't arrest her, because she hadn't done anything wrong—although technically she had kidnapped a child. Instinct told him to keep her out of the system, or the chief would find her for sure.

He found the gun, shoved it into the back of his waistband and turned.

Something smashed against his head.

He fell to the cold, hard snow, and blinked to clear his vision.

He was being dragged across the parking lot toward the Dumpster.

As they released him with a jerk, two men started kicking Matt. Was this a random mugging or had the chief's men found him? Did Billings suspect Matt knew more than he was saying?

"Where is she?" a man asked, delivering a kick to Matt's stomach.

"Who?" he gasped.

A solid boot jammed against his neck. He grabbed the guy's ankle and yanked.

The guy went down.

Matt scrambled to his feet.

The second guy snapped a cord around Matthew's neck, cutting off air. After surviving two tours in Afghanistan, dodging IEDs and defending innocents, he was going down like this?

God, if I'm done, I'm okay with that. But please protect Jenna and the child.

With a sudden release, he was shoved headfirst into the metal Dumpster, then yanked back and thrown onto the pavement. Drifting in and out of consciousness, all he could think about was Jenna, her colorful green eyes and lovely smile.

"Jenna North," the husky guy said, his face close to Matt's. "Where. Is. She?"

"Hang on, he's calling," the other guy said. "Yeah… Where? On our way. Let's go."

"What about the janitor?"

"Forget him. We've got a location on the woman."

On Jenna? They knew she was inside? Matt struggled to get up. One of the guys kicked him twice in the ribs for good measure.

Matt coughed and clutched his chest. With blurry vision, he watched the men cross the lot.

He had to get to her. Had to warn her.

Struggling to get up, his head spun and he collapsed on the pavement. He coached himself to breathe, to think past the throbbing headache long enough to help Jenna.

An innocent woman protecting an innocent child.

"Matthew?"

He looked up. Vivid green eyes sparkled down at him. Jenna.

No, they'd find her; they'd kill her. "You need to…"

What? Be taken into FBI custody? Why? He was in no shape to protect her, and by the time backup arrived, the thugs would have surely found her.

"My keys." He dug into his jacket pocket and fished them out. As he offered them to her, they slipped through his trembling fingers. "Take the truck. Get out of here."

He heard the keys scrape against the pavement. Good, she was taking his advice. Looking out for herself and the child.

A few seconds passed, maybe minutes—he couldn't be sure. What he did know was that if the cops found him, they'd ask questions, risking his cover.

Then again, he could tell the truth, to a point. He'd been jumped and beaten, and when he regained consciousness, his truck was gone.

"Open your eyes."

It was Jenna's voice.

He blinked a few times and found himself looking up at her beautiful face.

"You need to go," he ordered.

"Can you get up?"

"The men—"

"They're gone. Come on—stand up."

"Gone?" he said as she helped him to his feet. He groaned, clutching his ribs.

"They left. I called 9-1-1 and told them I was at Scooter's Pancake House in Cedar River."

"What about…the little boy?"

"He's in the car."

He blinked to clear the stars from his vision, but it didn't help much. Safe to say the chief's thugs had gifted him with a doozy of a concussion. When he reached his truck, Jenna led him to the passenger side.

"I'll drive," he said.

"You can barely stand. Get in." She glanced nervously over her shoulder. A few people inside the truck stop were watching from the window.

As he started to argue, he realized how right she was. Matt was in no shape to drive and they needed to get out of here, quick. The concussion was messing with his judgment. He'd have to rely on Jenna's acumen for the time being.

Once inside the truck, he closed his eyes. He heard her get behind the wheel, but she didn't start the vehicle.

He cracked open his eyes. "What…what's happening?"

"I need to take my contacts out." She dug through her bag.

"Do it when we're safe."

"I'll do it now, thank you very much," she snapped.

He'd made her angry. Why? He was trying to protect her, get her away from danger.

She pulled out a small container, and before he could say Miranda rights, she'd removed her contacts and was transformed with the help of large, dark-rimmed glasses. Her auburn hair had been tucked into a ski cap.

"Okay, let's take care of you. Where's the first aid kit?" she said.

"I'm fine." As he said the words, he found himself drifting into that dark place—the place between consciousness and sleep, the place where time didn't exist. Distant memories flooded his brain, memories of laughter, then anger…

A casket being lowered into the ground.

Sarah.

A gentle hand pressed a gauze pad against the side of his head. "Shh, hold still."

It was a firm voice, tinged with sweetness and concern. Who was it again? He'd distanced himself from relationships because of his work, his dedication to the job.

He'd attempted commitment with Sarah. And she was dead.

His fault.

There wasn't a day that went by when he didn't pray for forgiveness.

Shutting down the romantic part of his life was what had made him a good agent, an agent willing to devote all his energy into nailing criminals, men who pretended to be heroes, when they were actually…

He was falling again, floating like a leaf dropping from a tree. Where would he land? Back at her funeral? His remorse strangling him as he pleaded with God for forgiveness?

"It's okay. You're okay."

"Sarah?" he said.

"Almost done."

"I'm sorry."

An hour later, Jenna glanced at her passenger and wondered if she should take him to a hospital. His skin was pale and he groaned in his sleep every few minutes. Plus, he'd been having delusions back at the truck stop when she'd bandaged his head wound.

He'd whispered the name *Sarah*. His girlfriend? Wife?

"Stay focused," she said softly. She couldn't afford to be distracted by her passenger's nightmares. She needed to strategize what to do next, other than to distance herself from Cedar River.

"Stay back," Matthew muttered in his sleep.

Jenna suspected he had a concussion and knew the best treatment for that was sleep. She'd learned as much when she'd ended up in the hospital after one of her "falls."

She clenched her jaw. This was not the time, nor the place, to be thinking about the past. She had two people to protect—Little Eli and…an FBI agent. Which begged the question, why was he working undercover as a janitor at the community center?

"Medic," he said. He jerked awake, eyes wide, breathing heavily.

"Hey, you're okay," she said.

He glanced at her with a dazed expression.

"Just a bad dream," she said.

He snapped his attention away, as if embarrassed, and directed his gaze to the road ahead.

"Best thing for a concussion is sleep," she offered.

A moment later he closed his eyes. Wow, that surprised her. She thought she'd get more of an argument, or a lecture about how she should have left him back at the truck stop.

Why didn't you abandon him, Jenna?

Because of the vulnerability in his dulled blue eyes. She couldn't leave a semiconscious man lying on the cold, wet ground. After all, once the thugs figured out Jenna had diverted them from her true location, they would have returned to the truck stop and done even more damage to Matthew. He was in no position to defend himself.

She'd been in survival mode back at the office, driven by the trauma of her past. The chief's actions solidified her opinion of law enforcement, and her cautious nature had made her draw the conclusion that Matthew was a serial criminal, not a cop. Even if he was a cop, she knew they had their own code, and the normal rules of civility didn't apply to them.

Which left her in that same, familiar spot: alone and afraid.

And she couldn't afford to be afraid, not while Eli was in her care.

If only she had a burner phone to call Marcus again, get Eli safely to his cousin. Deep down, Jenna feared she was the absolute worst choice to protect Eli. She'd failed miserably before. What made her think this time would be different?

Her brain started clicking off options. What about… She glanced at her passenger. Could she risk getting help from the FBI? No, they'd force her to return Eli to his father, a man Chloe had called a *monster*. She shook off the thought.

The word *monster* taunted her, reminding her that although she was legally free of him, there were days she still felt like she was under Anthony's thumb, especially when she'd come home to her Cedar River apartment and find things out of place. She'd be yanked back into the past, experiencing Anthony's wrath over her unacceptable housekeeping skills. She'd try to shake it off, reminding herself she'd been in a hurry to get to work in the morning and had forgotten to put things where they belonged.

But the fear of punishment was quite real.

Move on, she coached herself.

She needed to think her way out of this current crisis, not be paralyzed by the past. Who could she go to for help? Jenna had been estranged from her family ever since she'd married Anthony, and had never reunited with them after she'd escaped his abuse. Distancing herself from everyone, past and present, had been the best way to put the horror behind her and live a safe life. She was willing to do whatever was necessary to achieve that goal, and starting a new life where no one knew her seemed like the only way.

A new life where she could be a different person. A stronger person.

She reconsidered calling Patrice. The middle-aged woman was devoted to helping victims flee dangerous situations. No, she had already put herself in enough danger for Jenna, although maybe Patrice could offer some advice.

The flash of blue and red lights sparked through the truck's rearview mirror. Jenna's heart leaped into her throat.

They'd found her.

THREE

"License and registration, please," a deep male voice said.

Matt forced his eyes open. He was in the passenger seat, and a uniformed officer stood at the driver's window.

"I'm sorry, Officer, was I speeding?" Jenna asked from behind the wheel of Matt's truck.

Jenna North was driving his truck?

"No, ma'am, but your left taillight is out," the cop said.

"Oh, thank you for letting us know."

"You're welcome. I'd still like to see your license and registration."

Jenna nodded at Matt, who read fear in her green eyes.

"Honey, can you get the registration?" she said.

Honey? Why was she calling him honey? And why did his head feel like someone had used it as a soccer ball?

"Sir, are you all right?" The cop aimed his flashlight into the vehicle.

Matt put up his hand to block the piercing beam. "My head," is all that came out.

"We're on the way to the hospital," Jenna said. "He was mugged and has a head injury."

The cop nodded, speculative. He started to aim the beam into the back seat.

"Please don't wake the baby," she said.

The baby? *What have you gotten yourself into, Matt?*

"I still need to see your license and registration," the cop said.

She pulled her license out of her wallet. Matt dug the registration out of the glove box and passed it, and his license, to the officer.

"Did you file a police report about the mugging?" the officer asked, scanning the registration.

"We will, Officer, but I wanted to get him checked out first," she said in a frantic tone.

Jenna North, development manager of the Broadlake Foundation, was worried about Matt.

What had happened to him?

His mind drew a blank. He'd obviously lost the past few, what, hours? Days? The amnesia had to be related to the headache clawing its way across his skull. He was suffering from a concussion. But how had it happened?

Bigger question—why did he have an urgent need to protect Miss North and…a baby?

He looked over his shoulder. There was a sleeping child in the back seat. Whose? Jenna's? No, she wasn't married, didn't have a boyfriend or even date, if you believed the locals. She was a transplant from Tulsa with a generous heart, a woman who used her social and financial talents to raise money for the Broadlake Foundation.

"Please wait here," the cop said and left them alone.

Jenna turned to Matt. "They're going to find us. What do we do?"

She could tell him what was going on, for starters.

"Matthew?"

The way she spoke his name made it sound like they were close, like they knew each other outside of working in the same building. Sure, he might have imagined dating someone like Jenna, a lovely woman determined to help people. Only he didn't remember ever grabbing coffee with her or chatting outside of work. He was on the job and, even if he weren't, he'd made a promise to himself to avoid romantic entanglements.

"What's he doing?" she said, eyeing the rearview mirror.

"Patience," he said. "He's running the registration. It's procedure."

He closed his eyes, fighting back the anxiety

taunting him. He'd have to confess his condition because he needed her help to navigate through the temporary amnesia. Matt sensed she needed his help as well.

"Aren't you worried?" she asked.

He opened his eyes, but couldn't admit the truth: that he was terrified because he'd lost a chunk of time.

"No, of course you're not worried, you're FBI," she muttered and studied the rearview.

She knew the truth? Which meant what—that she was helping with the investigation? Was that possible? Because he didn't remember her being ruled out as a suspect.

He needed to remember.

"He's coming back," she said, sitting straight.

The officer, who Matt realized was a state trooper, stepped up to her window and passed her the licenses and registration. "The closest medical facility is St. James Healthcare. I'll escort you."

"We wouldn't want to take you away from your duties, Officer," she said.

"You're not. Follow me."

She closed the window and sighed. "Now what?" she asked Matt. "Should I ditch him?"

"Ditch him?" he repeated in a sarcastic tone.

"Bad idea, huh?"

"Pretty bad, yeah."

"What if he called Billings? What if he's on

their payroll? What if they're waiting at the hospital? What if—"

"Slow down, speedy. You're making my headache worse."

"Sorry, sorry." The squad car passed them and she followed. "I wish I could get ahold of Marcus."

"Who's Marcus?"

"Chloe's cousin. He's supposed to help."

"Ma'am?"

"What?" She shot him a quick glance.

"Chloe...?"

"Mrs. McFadden," she said. "You remember."

Mrs. McFadden—sure, he knew her. She was on the development board and helped with fundraising events. All roads to the money-laundering investigation led to Mrs. McFadden's husband, Gary, but they didn't have enough to build a case. They'd even considered that his wife might be involved.

"Matthew?" she said.

"Yes, ma'am?"

"What's going on?"

"I'm having some...memory challenges."

"Oh."

He heard the disappointment in her voice, as if she'd been relying on him to protect her and the child. But that hadn't been his assignment. His assignment was to work as a custodian in the foundation office, be invisible and gather information. Keep an eye on nighttime activity, determine if they were not only laundering money for the cartel but were also distributing drugs out of the community center.

"Blows to the head can do that," she offered. "Don't freak out. It's usually temporary."

"How would you know that?"

She shrugged. There was more to it, but she wasn't sharing. Why would she? She was stuck with a helpless man and…a child.

"So, the child is Mrs. McFadden's?" he asked.

"Yes."

"Where is Mrs. McFadden?"

She gripped the steering wheel with white-knuckled fingers.

"Miss North?" he prompted.

"Jenna, call me Jenna," she said, with slight irritation in her voice.

"Okay, Jenna. Why is Mrs. McFadden's child in my truck?"

"She asked me to protect him."

"I don't understand."

"Chief Billings killed Chloe," she blurted out in a pained voice.

He glanced out the passenger window and fisted his hand to stop his fingers from trembling. Men like Matt didn't tremble, and they didn't let fear run rampant. Yet this was the first time he'd awakened with a chunk of his life missing, like it had never happened, and he was forced to rely on a stranger to fill in the blanks.

Well, not a complete stranger. He'd done a background check on all the foundation employees to help identify which ones were the most likely to be involved in the money-laundering activity. Matt still couldn't wrap his head around the fact that all roads led to the small, quaint town of Cedar River, Montana, known for its world-class scones and snow sports, headquarters of the international and altruistic Broadlake Foundation.

His supervisor had gotten Matt a job as the night custodian, and during the day he continued surveillance at the hot spots in town. They suspected money was being filtered through the foundation in the form of donations, only they couldn't determine who was orchestrating the mystery deposits into the accounts. Everyone had been suspect, even the town's police chief, who was on the governing board.

If what Jenna said was true, it confirmed Chief Billings's involvement. Matt didn't remember seeing the murder, but Jenna had.

Which meant she was a key witness—and her life was in serious danger.

He'd always sensed wariness about Jenna, even though she covered it with a bright smile and polite manners. His job required him to pay attention to the little things, the way her shoulders jerked at unexpected sounds and how she'd clenched her jaw when a drunk, homeless man wandered into the center and refused to leave. Matt had come to her rescue that night, escorting him outside and waiting for Kyle to take the belligerent man into custody.

Something had happened to Jenna North that didn't show up on a routine background check. Yet it seemed like she'd lived an unremarkable life before moving to Cedar River.

He tapped a closed fist against his knee. How could he remember details about Miss North's background but couldn't remember what happened to him in the past...what? How much time had he lost?

"Can you please tell me what happened tonight?" he said.

"What's the last thing you remember?"

He closed his eyes. "The Avalanche were winning. I was in my office listening to the game."

"You don't remember Chloe screaming?"

"No, ma'am."

"Or finding me outside with Eli?"

"No. I need to figure out how much time I've lost."

She recounted what happened in the last hour, starting with her friend being strangled, Jenna asking Matt to drop her at the truck stop and then her coming to his rescue after he was assaulted in the parking lot.

"That's pretty much it," she said.

Not quite. "I left you at the truck stop when I knew you were in danger? That doesn't sound like me."

"A misunderstanding." She hesitated. "I thought you were a serial killer."

He shot her a look of disbelief.

"What? You had a gun, zip ties and duct tape in your glove box."

"The gun and zip ties are for work. I used the duct tape to fix a broken hose."

"Oh, okay. Sorry," she said.

"Trusting doesn't come easy for you, does it?"

"I trusted Chloe," she said quietly.

Silence stretched between them.

"Why were you working undercover at the community center?" she asked.

How much should he tell her? He knew she needed enough information to make good decisions.

"We think a drug cartel is laundering money through the foundation," he said. "By taking a job at the center and assimilating into the community, my goal was to discover who's involved."

"Assimilating into the community?"

"Through work, volunteering, attending church."

"That seems hypocritical, to pretend to attend church."

"I wasn't pretending. I enjoy church."

"Whatever."

He'd upset her but wasn't sure why. He'd figure that out later. In the meantime, he'd call for backup. He searched his pocket for his phone but came up empty.

"Your phone's in the console," she said.

He looked at her.

"You dropped it when they attacked you."

"Thanks."

"And here, you'll probably need this." She pulled his gun magazine out of her pocket and handed it to him.

He took it, trying to figure out why she had it.

"I thought you were a serial killer, remember?" she said.

"Right." He pulled the gun out of his waistband, shoved the magazine in place and put it in the glove box.

"You're not keeping it on you?"

"It'll raise questions in the hospital and I don't want to jeopardize my assignment."

"Oh, right."

Matt called his supervisor, pressing the heel of his palm against his temple to ease the pain. It went to voice mail. "It's Weller. I was assaulted and need backup. Send an agent to St. James Healthcare in Butte. I'm with a woman and child who need our protection." He pocketed his phone and leaned against the headrest.

"You don't have to take care of us," Jenna said.

"Excuse me?"

"We're not your problem."

"No, you're not my problem. You're my responsibility."

She smirked and looked away. Why? She didn't know anything about Matt. She didn't know how he'd failed Sarah.

"I'd like to find Chloe's cousin to help us, not be taken into FBI custody," she said.

"I'm trying to keep you safe."

She shook her head, unconvinced. Man, what had happened to this woman?

A few minutes later they exited the highway, and she turned into the hospital parking lot. "Do you want me to drop you at the main entrance?" she offered.

"No, we should stick together until help arrives."

She found a parking spot, turned off the vehicle and tried to hand him the keys.

"Keep them. Just in case."

"I can't take your truck."

"For my peace of mind."

With a curious frown, she got out of the car and retrieved the sleeping child. His head rested on her shoulder as she carried him through the parking lot.

"Want me to carry him?" he offered.

"You've got a concussion. You shouldn't be carrying anything."

Good point, which just went to show that his

brain was muddled. As they approached the hospital, the state trooper joined them. "I've gotta go. When you're done being treated, call this number." He handed Matt a business card. "They'll send someone to take your statement."

"Thanks," Matt said.

The cop turned to Jenna. "Ma'am, don't worry. They'll take good care of your husband."

When Jenna didn't correct the "husband" remark, Matt glanced at her. She looked like she was about to burst into tears. Why? Because she was worried about Matt's condition? No, something else was going on.

"Thanks again, Officer," Matt said, and motioned Jenna inside.

Once they were seated in the waiting area, he noticed her hand trembling as she stroked the little boy's back.

"It'll be okay," Matt offered. "Help's on the way."

No reaction. She didn't nod, shrug or even roll her eyes. She continued to stare straight ahead with a dazed look on her face.

"Jenna?"

She seemed lost in another world, as if she was having a flashback, and not a good one. He touched her arm that held the boy against her shoulder. She didn't look at him. The child was asleep, sucking on a pacifier and clinging to his stuffed bear.

Matt slid a chair in front of her and blocked her view. “Jenna, look at me.”

She blinked, and her wounded green eyes connected with Matt’s. It felt like he’d been slugged in the gut.

“You’re okay,” he said.

“I… I don’t like hospitals.”

“What happened?” he asked.

“I’m sorry?”

“To make you not like hospitals?”

She took a deep breath, opened her mouth and closed it again. Then she said, “I got hurt.”

The way she articulated those three words reminded him of a little girl who’d fallen on the playground. But Jenna wasn’t a little girl, and he suspected she’d suffered a lot worse than a skinned knee.

“You’re not hurt now,” he said, gently squeezing her shoulder. “You’re A-okay.”

She was more than okay in Matt’s eyes. This woman was strong, smart and determined to do the right thing, to protect her friend’s child.

“I won’t be okay until this little boy is safe with his cousin.” The fear in her eyes turned to anger.

“I understand, but I need to ask you something. What about the boy’s father? I mean, at this point you could be accused of kidnapping.”

“His mother begged me to protect Eli, especially from Gary. What would you have me do, hand him over to an abusive father?”

"Of course not, but there are laws and procedures for cases like this."

"What about the law for murder? Or does that not apply to cops? The police are obviously involved, so excuse me if I don't have much faith in the law."

"If Chief Billings killed—"

"If? You don't believe me?"

"I do, but we need more than your word. In the meantime, we have to protect you and the little boy. My people can help."

"Cops won't help me."

"The chief is one bad cop out of what, twenty on the Cedar River Police force? That doesn't mean they're all bad." *That I'm bad.*

"Chloe's husband is wealthy. I'm sure he can make them bad by throwing money at them."

"You're awfully cynical for such a young woman."

"Well, at least I'm not dead."

That comment stopped him cold. Was she referring to her friend or herself? Had someone threatened Jenna's life, putting her in the hospital?

"Mr. Weller?" a nurse said from the examining room door.

He put up his hand, indicating he'd heard her. Matt studied Jenna. "Will you come in with me?"

She looked at him but didn't answer.

“I don’t want to leave you and the child alone,” he said.

With a nod, she stood and accompanied him into the examining area.

Jenna managed to keep Eli comfortable and asleep, Bubba the bear wedged firmly between the child’s cheek and Jenna’s shoulder. As the doctor put a few stitches in Matthew’s head wound and examined his other injuries—bruised ribs and a reddened cheek—she struggled to distance herself from the situation. Not easy when she was surrounded by the smells, sights and sounds that triggered violent memories.

Her left eye swollen shut.

Pain piercing across her torso every time she drew a breath.

Knowing that she’d lost her baby, even before the doctor had told her.

As she rocked with Eli in her arms, she decided she had to get out of this hospital before she completely lost it and burst into uncontrollable tears.

Snap out of it. Stop thinking about yourself, and focus on the little boy.

“Want me to hold him?” Matt asked.

She glanced up. They were alone in the examining area. The doctor and nurse had left and she hadn’t even noticed. She must pay more attention to her surroundings.

“Are you ready to go?” she said.

"Not quite. The nurse is getting me an ice bag and ibuprofen to take home." He shook his head. "Home? What am I talking about?" he muttered.

"How's your… Did you tell them about your memory?"

"No. Didn't want to give them a reason to admit me."

"Maybe they should do a CT scan."

"Not necessary. You're not the only one who's suffered a concussion before."

She sensed his comment was meant to be an opening for her to share more about herself. But that was not happening. Ever. The shame would choke her before the words passed her lips.

"It will be okay," Matthew said.

He was offering comfort because he sensed how stressed she was, how nervous and maybe even terrified about what would happen next. The list of options flashed across her mind—she'd be arrested for kidnapping; Eli would be handed back to his abusive father and Jenna would be imprisoned for trying to save a child; or worse—she'd be found by Chief Billings.

The image of Chloe's lifeless body dropping to the floor sent shockwaves of fear all the way to her fingertips. The little boy sighed and stirred against her shoulder. It gave her strength.

She stood. "I'm glad you're okay, Matthew."

"I hear a *but* at the end of that sentence."

"I need to find Chloe's cousin Marcus."

"We can help with that."

"But you won't, will you? You'll be required to place Eli back with his father."

"As I said, if you have proof that he is harming the child—"

"Chloe's word is enough for me."

"I understand, but it may not be enough for the law."

"The law." She couldn't stop a sardonic chuckle from escaping her lips. "I don't care about the law. I care about protecting this little boy."

"I can't let you leave." He shifted off the exam table.

Panic shot through her body. Not again. She couldn't deal with another domineering man.

You'll never leave me.

Her mind whirred with options as she clung tighter to Eli. Why had she trusted Matthew?

"Jenna?" he said.

She stared across the room at an IV stand, planning her escape. He placed his hand on her shoulder. She nearly jerked away, but didn't want to upset the child.

"Don't touch me," she ground out.

He withdrew his hand and studied her.

"I'm trying to help," he said. "I don't want you to be arrested for kidnapping."

She was about to fire back a retort when the nurse returned with an ice bag and pain reliever.

"Everything okay?" she asked, glancing from Matthew to Jenna.

No, it wasn't okay. She'd been trapped in a cage again, unable to break free.

"We're good," Matt said.

"Someone's asking for you out front," the nurse said to him and left.

As he headed for the door, he turned to Jenna. "Wait here."

What did that mean? That he didn't trust his own people—the agent who was asking for him?

The moment he left the examining room, she grabbed the diaper and messenger bags. There was an exit on the other side of the room. Perfect.

Was she overreacting? No, Matthew's comment about custody and giving this precious child back to his father had strengthened Jenna's resolve to keep Eli safe and away from that monster.

A monster like Jenna's ex.

I can't let you leave. Matthew's words came back to her. Did he belong in the monster category as well?

Holding Eli against her shoulder, she went to the door and cracked it open to determine the positions of Matthew and the agent. The waiting area was empty. Strange.

"I can't help you, sir," a receptionist said. There was something in her voice…

Fear.

Jenna cracked the door a little wider. She spotted two things simultaneously—Matthew on the floor, and a man, wearing all black, pointing a gun at the receptionist.

Jenna snapped out of view. It wasn't one of the men from the community center. Which meant there was a whole army of thugs looking for her and Eli?

Struggling against fear that threatened to consume her, she rushed to the other door, swung it open and started down the back hall. She had to get away. Find Marcus. Get this child into the hands of someone who could protect him.

Guilt snagged her conscience. She'd brought danger into a hospital full of innocent staff members and patients.

The minute she and Eli were safely away, she'd call police about the gunman in the lobby.

"Stop right there," a male voice demanded.

FOUR

Jenna froze, her heart pounding in her ears.

She gripped Eli tighter, whispering against his knit hat, "I'm sorry, sweetie."

No, don't you dare give up.

"I'm sorry, but I can't let you leave," the man said.

Did he just say *I'm sorry*?

She turned and was relieved to see a hospital security officer walking toward her.

"There's a man with a gun—"

"Take it easy." He put out his right hand as he approached, like he was calming a wild stallion. His left hand rested on a club at his hip.

"In the lobby—a gunman is threatening your staff."

In a placating tone he said, "I need you to come with me."

Her gaze darted toward Matthew's exam room. Any second now the thug would figure out Jenna was close, and he'd come bursting through the door.

"Please, ma'am," the security officer, a gray-haired man in his midsixties, said.

Every inch of her body screamed to get out of here. If she ran she wouldn't get far, with two bags strapped across her shoulders and clutching a toddler in her arms. The security guy would chase after her, probably sound the alarm, drawing even more attention to Jenna and Eli's presence.

"Why do I need to come with you?" she said.

He sighed and took his hand off the club resting at his hip. "I received an informal request to keep an eye out for a young woman and a child who went missing from Cedar River."

"That's not me."

"Then I'm sure we can clear it up quickly. Please, I need you to come to my office."

The problem was, his office was in the same building where a kidnapper—probably more than one—was looking for Jenna and Eli.

"Let's go," he said.

Refusing would make her look guilty. All she needed to do was act innocent and agreeable, and once he went to check on the situation out front she'd sneak away.

With a nod, she walked alongside him, fearing he'd pull out cuffs, but he didn't. Of course not—he wouldn't cuff a woman carrying a child.

As he led her down the hall, her instincts remained on full alert, and her mind calculated options, solutions. When they made a left turn, she spotted an exit up ahead. Not wanting to give away her thoughts, she turned her attention to Eli, whispering sweet words against his cheek, acting like a loving mom.

A sharp pain lanced through her chest and she shoved it aside. She had to convince the guard she was Eli's mother, not some crazy woman who'd kidnapped a child.

He opened the door to his office and motioned to a chair beside his desk. "I'll be back shortly."

"Aren't you going to call the police about the gunman out front?"

"I'll check it out."

"No, he's dangerous, he's—"

He shut the door on her protest. Foolish man—he wasn't capable of dealing with these violent criminals.

She grabbed the doorknob and twisted. It was locked.

Shaking her head, she fought the frustration welling up inside for letting herself be caught, locked up. For all she knew, the request to keep an eye out for her had come directly from Chief Billings with a generous finder's fee attached.

She needed to get out of here. She needed help.

Grabbing the office phone, she found an outside line and called 9-1-1 to report the gunman because either the guard was an accomplice, or he was making a dangerous mistake by confronting the man.

Then she called Patrice.

"Hello?" the older woman answered.

"It's Jenna." She put it on speaker.

"What's wrong?"

"I'm sorry to be calling."

"You never have to apologize to me. How can I help?"

"My friend was murdered and I'm watching her little boy, and now they're after him too, after us, and—"

"Take a breath."

She paused, inhaled a deep breath and exhaled.

"If you want to think clearly you need to be calm, lower your heart rate and get grounded, remember?"

"Yes."

"What's the immediate danger?"

"I'm locked in a security guard's office at a hospital and I can't get out."

"Yes, you can. Look for paper clips, something to use on the lock."

"If I get out of here—"

"When you get out of there?"

"When I get out of here, I may need your help again."

"There's always room for you at the cabin, Jenna, you know that. Now look for paper clips.

Who knows, you might find a spare office key in his desk drawer."

She did her best to one-handedly search drawers, thankful that Eli was sound asleep against her shoulder.

"You're caring for a little boy?" Patrice asked.

"Yes."

"How old?"

"Eighteen months."

A knowing silence filled the line.

"I'm okay," Jenna assured her friend.

"Where is he now?"

"I'm holding him."

"They have these nifty baby carriers that you strap to your body. The motion soothes the child and it would make carrying him a lot easier. You can pick one up when you get out of there."

"Okay."

"What's his name?"

"Eli," she said, sifting through a top drawer. "He's a super good boy." She found a tray of paper clips. "Do you really think I can—?"

Someone rattled the doorknob.

Jenna spun around. "They're trying to get in."

"Can you find something to defend yourself with?"

Jenna grabbed scissors and hit the off button on the phone, not wanting Patrice to hear what might happen next. Because Jenna would surely die before handing this innocent child over to killers.

She swallowed back her fear, gripping the child with one arm while clutching the scissors with her other hand.

The door unlocked with a click.

"Jenna, it's me," Matthew said before entering the office.

He opened the door…

To the sight of Jenna wielding eight-inch scissors in her hand.

He anticipated she'd be panicked, which is why he announced himself. He also knew she'd probably commit assault in order to protect the child.

"Let's go," he said, ignoring her terrified expression and the white-knuckled grip of the weapon.

She didn't move at first.

"We've gotta get out of here, and I mean yesterday." He motioned with his hands. "Is the baby okay?"

That seemed to redirect her attention. She glanced at the child leaning against her shoulder. "Yes, he's fine."

"Good, then let's go."

She started toward the door.

"I don't think you'll need the scissors."

She glanced at her hand.

"Unless you want to bring them, which is fine. We've gotta make tracks here, Jenna."

"Right, of course." She dropped the scissors

on the desk and followed Matt. "I saw you on the floor. That man with a gun, and then..." She glanced at him with a question in her eyes.

"I was able to neutralize him."

"So the security guard wasn't working with him?"

"No. I flashed my ID and told him the woman and child who accompanied me to the hospital were being taken into protective custody."

They reached the exit and she hesitated.

"What?" he said.

"I won't let them take Eli away from me." She took a step backward. "I won't return him to his father."

"I know, and I understand. Right now I need to get you and Eli safe. That's all I'm concerned with. I'm not sure I can trust my own people at this point. But you and me? We have to trust each other. What do I need to do to make you trust me, Jenna?"

"You won't take him back to his father?"

"No."

Matt had just made a promise, one that might require him to break the law. He didn't know what compelled him to say it, but he had to get Jenna and the child out of here. He doubted the guy out front was alone.

She studied him with that contemplative look of hers. "Fine. I'll try trusting you."

"You'll try?" he said, pushing open the door.

"I haven't had much success trusting people."

He guided her through the back lot, his gaze assessing, searching for signs of trouble. "Have a little faith."

"Haven't had much success in that department either," she said softly.

He couldn't look at her, didn't want to see the devastating sadness he knew would be reflected in her eyes.

"Was that guy working for the chief?" she asked.

"That would be my guess."

"And you think someone at the FBI gave him our location?"

"I can't rule it out. You have my keys?"

"You sure you should drive?"

"I'm better now, thanks."

She passed them to Matt. The brief contact shot warmth up his arm.

They walked in silence—a good thing because he wanted to evaluate their surroundings and the danger that could be waiting for them. Three squad cars were speeding toward the hospital. He shifted her behind him and hesitated. "That should keep everyone busy so they don't see us leave."

"Where are we going?"

"Someplace safe."

Without looking at her, he gently placed his

hand on her arm, and this time she didn't pull away. He guided her toward the truck.

Officers rushed into the ER entrance, where he hoped they'd arrest the gunman, whom Matt had fastened with the security guard's cuffs to a desk. Matt still wasn't sure how he'd found the physical energy to subdue the guy.

But he didn't need to wonder for long. He was focused on Jenna and the little boy, on making sure they were safe.

Jenna quickly buckled Eli in his car seat and climbed into the passenger seat, and Matt pulled out.

Neither of them spoke for a good ten minutes, almost as if they were both still holding their breath, waiting for the next attack.

"What happened back there?" she finally asked.

"The gunman had everyone cornered and ordered me down. It didn't look good. Then the security guard showed up, distracting the gunman, and I tackled him without incident."

"With a concussion and bruised ribs?" she said with awe in her voice.

"Once I cuffed the guy, the guard said you'd told him about the shooter, that you were locked in his office. I assumed it was for your own safety."

"No, the guard said someone informally requested he keep an eye out for a woman who'd kidnapped a child from Cedar River."

"At least it's not an official BOLO," he muttered.

With a nod, she gazed out her window. She looked so...lost.

"You were smart to try to escape once you saw what was going on in the waiting room," he said, trying to offer encouragement. He glanced at her, but she didn't look proud. She seemed ashamed. "What's that look?"

She shook her head.

"Jenna? We've got to trust each other, right?"

"The moment you left the examining room I was planning to escape."

"I don't understand. You didn't know—"

"I was scared of you."

He gripped the steering wheel tighter. "Scared. Of me?"

"Yes." She fiddled with a silver ring on her right hand.

"You're going to have to explain that. Please."

"As you've probably guessed, I have a rather tragic past."

Tragic. The word conjured all kinds of images, images he struggled to ignore.

"I've made some foolish choices I wish I could take back, but I can't."

He waited patiently, wanting her to feel comfortable enough to share her story at her own pace.

"The last time I was in a hospital," she said with hesitation, "my ex-husband put me there."

Things started to make sense: her anxious behavior and the wariness in her eyes. Especially around men.

Even around Matt.

Regret whipped through him.

"I would never hurt you, Jenna."

"Well, whenever I'm in a situation that reminds me of Anthony, I get sucked into the past and feel those same feelings."

"Does that happen often?" he asked.

"No." She glanced at him. "But it's happened a few times since Chloe's murder."

"Understandable. What did I do at the hospital to make you want to run?"

"You stood up to overpower me."

He glanced at her, but she wouldn't make eye contact. Was she still afraid?

"I… I'm sorry," he said.

"What?"

"I'm sorry if my behavior upset you. That was not my intention."

"You said…you said that you wouldn't let me leave."

He had spoken those words, but because he wanted to protect her. Still, he knew that arguing with her wouldn't help to develop the trust he wanted to cultivate between them.

"And that reminded me of Anthony, the things he used to say to me."

"Like what?"

"That's personal."

"If I'm to avoid upsetting you, I'd like to know where the land mines are."

She hugged herself and sighed. "He'd say that he loved me so much he devoted his life to being a good husband. Then it turned into he devoted his life to protecting me, mostly from myself because of my bad choices. After a while you start to believe the lies. One night I'd finally had enough and stood up to him."

Matt could tell she was reliving the incident. "What happened?"

"He grabbed my shoulders and shook me until I could hardly think, then he threw me aside." She glanced at Matt. "That was the last time I ended up in the hospital."

"The last time? You mean there were other times?"

She hugged herself tighter, but didn't answer.

"Didn't you call the police?" he said.

"Why? He donated to the police chief's political campaign to run for mayor. He was friendly with a few of the local detectives. It was pointless to reach out to them for help. Besides, Anthony always had this way of promising it would get better. He went to anger management therapy, and for a while he'd be the loving husband I thought I'd married. It never lasted."

"So you got a divorce? You escaped?"

"With a lot of help. A woman came to see me in the hospital. She challenged me to stand up for myself. That's when my fight for freedom began."

"How did you get away?"

"There's a group that helps women like me. I can't share the details. They need to remain anonymous."

"I understand."

"Do you? You're a man in a powerful profession. You can take away someone's freedom, question their backgrounds, their decisions."

"It's my job to protect—"

"Funny, that's what Anthony used to say. It was his job to take care of me. His job to protect me."

Another awkward silence stretched between them. Matt didn't think it wise to point out he was nothing like her former husband. Posttrauma triggers weren't always rational, but they were definitely painful, and all too real.

"I'm glad you got away from him," he offered.

"I'm not sure I have."

"What do you mean?"

"Here I am on the run again, fighting for my life, and the life of a little boy."

"This is different."

"Whatever. I guess I have to accept the fact that I will repeat my mistakes and will end up living under a cloud of violence. That's just my fate."

"Don't talk like that. You're in this situation because you're doing an honorable favor for your friend."

"Why would Chloe pick me? She had plenty of other friends she could have chosen."

"Maybe she didn't think they were as strong as you, or as nurturing."

When she swiped at her eye, he figured she was fighting back tears.

Way to go, Weller. Make the woman cry.

He redirected his attention to the dark highway, struggling to come up with what he should say to ease her pain. He didn't consider himself an expert at finding the right words to comfort someone, to encourage hope. Maybe if he'd been better at listening and offering compassion, Sarah wouldn't have left.

She wouldn't have driven so fast that she'd ended up dead. He should have been there for her. He could have saved her.

But he didn't.

And now the Lord had given him another chance, this time to save an emotionally wounded, yet strong woman—an innocent woman and a child.

Thank you, Lord, for entrusting me with this responsibility. I will not fail.

* * *

Trust.

As Jenna gazed out the window into the darkness, she considered the word and all its meaning. It certainly meant relying on someone, believing they had your best interest at heart.

Trust.

For Jenna, *trust* was like a muscle that had atrophied after years of nonuse. She couldn't remember the last time she'd trusted anyone, especially a man.

She'd trusted the members of Gloria's Guardians, the team that helped her escape Anthony. It had been the right choice. She knew if she'd stayed with her abusive husband—mostly out of fear—she probably wouldn't have made it to her next birthday.

The Guardians set everything up, including the plan to shut down Anthony. It started with the discussion she had with him at the hospital about the loss of their child. She'd recorded every word. It didn't take much to enrage him. It never did.

She hadn't expected him to say she'd deserved to be thrown down the stairs, which was basically a confession to fetal homicide. Just when she thought he might hit her again, two hospital security guards and her lawyer entered the room to intervene.

They had enough evidence to bring charges against Anthony. She didn't want to go through an ugly, painful trial, although she'd pretended to be up for the fight. Fearing she'd make a sympathetic witness, and knowing his own recorded admission would get him convicted, Anthony took a plea deal of three years and agreed to a quick divorce. He didn't want his sterling reputation to be tarnished, and apparently explained to friends that, although innocent, he'd spend the time in jail if it would help his fragile wife heal from the loss of their child.

What a master manipulator.

The Guardians had found her a powerful attorney to defend her pro bono, and even hired a security team to make sure Anthony couldn't intimidate or hurt her while out on bail.

Once he'd signed the divorce papers, the change of identity and relocation efforts began. For all intents and purposes, Anna Marie Brighton had vanished, never to be seen or heard from again.

At first, losing Joey had destroyed her.

Then it had given her incredible strength to fight back.

"How long ago?" Matt said.

She glanced at him. "I'm sorry?"

"When did you divorce your husband?"

After he committed murder.

"It's been a little over two years."

"In Tulsa?"

"No."

"But your background check—"

"You did a background check on me?"

"We were looking into everyone's backgrounds for links to suspicious activity at the Broadlake Foundation."

"What did you find out about me?"

"Other than that you're from Tulsa? Not much."

Her initial panic was quickly tempered with appreciation for the system that had saved her. If he thought she was from Tulsa rather than her true location, a suburb north of Chicago, then even federal agents couldn't see past her newly minted identity into her dark past.

"Who did that for you?" he asked. "Changed your background?"

She shot him a raised eyebrow.

"No, not so I can arrest them."

"I should hope not. There's nothing wrong with wanting to live a safe life away from your abuser."

"I agree."

"They only used first names to protect their identities, and those names could be pseudonyms. That reminds me, I should let my primary guardian know I'm okay. I was on the phone with her when you found me in the office. Wait, and there's another call I should make first. Can I use your phone?"

"You don't have one?"

"Thought it would be best to toss it."

He offered her his phone with a steady hand. Matt's recovery amazed Jenna. He'd been beaten up back at the truck stop, yet in the hour spent at the hospital, he seemed to have recovered quite well. She wondered if that meant he remembered anything about Chloe's murder.

"How are you feeling?" she asked.

"Frustrated."

"I mean physically—your head, your ribs?"

He shrugged. "Ibuprofen helped."

"And your memory?"

"No, I'm sorry." He seemed as disappointed as Jenna.

She found it interesting that even though he hadn't seen the murder, he trusted Jenna's word that it had happened.

Jenna called Marcus, but again it went to voice mail. "Can I leave him your number?" she asked.

"Sure." He gave it to her, and she repeated it on the message.

Then she called Patrice, who also didn't answer, so Jenna left a message. "Hey, it's Jenna. Sorry about not calling sooner. Things got a little crazy, but I'm okay. Thanks for being there, and keeping me sane. I'm using a friend's phone in case they've got a trace on my cell. I'll pick up a burner and call you tomorrow. Be well."

She ended the call and placed the phone on the dash holder.

"Sounds like you and this woman have become good friends."

"We have," she said. Even though Jenna sincerely wanted to trust Matt, she would never expose the team of mostly women to whom she owed her life.

To think, if she hadn't survived, she wouldn't be here today to protect baby Eli. She glanced into the back seat. He was sound asleep.

"He's a remarkably good boy," she said.

"Yeah, wait until he wakes up hungry. Then he'll let us have it."

"You have children?"

"No, but my brothers have a couple of kids. Is there food in the diaper bag?"

Jenna grabbed it off the floor and searched inside. "Cereal, crackers, fruit, a bottle and dry formula." She glanced at Matt. "Chloe was ready for anything."

"Or maybe she was planning to run."

They shared a look.

"That will get us through the morning. We'll pick up more supplies tomorrow," he said.

"You still haven't told me where we're going."

"There's a couple that offers their home to young women who are in trouble."

"You mean…?"

"Victims of abuse, human trafficking. They stay at Nancy and Ed Miller's farm for protection and to learn skills to help them move on."

"Kind of like the team that helped me."

"Yep. There are a lot of folks out there willing to help people who, by no fault of their own, have become victims."

She wondered if that was a not-so-subtle hint on his part that his motives were honorable.

"Are you sure the farm's a good place to take Eli?" she said.

"These women are victims too, Jenna," he said.

"I know, but aren't we putting them in danger by going there?"

"No one knows the location of the farm except for law enforcement, and the locals are good at protecting Nancy and Ed's altruistic work. Right now they only have one guest, so they've got plenty of room."

"You've spoken with them?"

"Texted. They'll leave a key in the planter box so we can let ourselves in."

His phone rang and he glanced at the number but didn't answer.

"Who is it?" Jenna asked.

"My boss. I'll call him back once we're safe."

That sounded like he wasn't one hundred percent sure they were out of danger.

Shivers trickled across her body. It wasn't until just now that the magnitude of the past few hours landed squarely on her shoulders.

She was still in danger. On the run. And this time it wasn't just about her.

A child depended on her—another innocent child.

"Jenna?" Matt said.

She glanced at him.

"I will protect you."

An hour later Matt's words still echoed in the silence between them. Jenna had gone quiet since he'd uttered the promise...again. He didn't know how many times he'd have to say it to convince her of his integrity and his goal: protecting Jenna and Eli.

Jenna, a witness to murder, who was on the run with another woman's child.

A dead woman's child.

Why couldn't he remember? He had to have seen something at the community center. He wanted desperately for the memory to return, but until the swelling went down in his brain, he was at the mercy of his injuries.

And the men who seemed to be constantly right behind him.

It was almost as if Billings's men knew where he was going to be before he got there. Nah, that was his concussion messing with him. He was overthinking things, acting paranoid, even a little confused.

But he wasn't confused about Jenna. She'd shut down, turning her face to the window as if to signal there was nothing more to talk about.

As if she didn't believe him when he pledged to protect her, and she wanted him to stop saying it.

Well, she'd better get used to it, because he'd keep repeating the promise until he read acceptance in her eyes.

Could he blame her for being cautious after everything she'd been though with an abusive former husband? He needed to be patient and offer more compassion.

He glanced in the rearview mirror for signs they were being followed. The road was empty for miles behind them. Then he caught sight of baby Eli. He hoped they could get him in the house and resettled without disturbing the child too much. Nancy would be thrilled to wake up tomorrow with a little one under her roof, since her youngest grandchild was in his teens.

Confident they weren't being followed, he turned onto the dirt road leading to the Millers' farm, the refuge for young women who'd been used and abused, a lot like Jenna.

He clenched his jaw, wondering what kind of jerk would abuse a lovely woman like Jenna North. A bully, no doubt, a man who had to pick on others to make himself feel strong.

"I'm sorry," he blurted out.

"What?" She turned to him.

"About your ex-husband, what he did to you."

"Me too."

"What happened to him?"

She crossed her arms over her chest. She clearly wasn't ready to share the details.

It was a defiant, determined gesture. He'd need that determination, along with a solid plan, to keep her safe. Tonight he just wanted to settle in, take time in a safe environment to strategize his next move.

They pulled up to the side of the house and parked. "Just give me a minute."

"It's kind of hard to trust you when I think you're going behind my back and saying who knows what to the people inside."

"I'm sure they're asleep, Jenna. I'm being extra careful and want to go in first to make sure it's safe."

"Oh." She fiddled with her silver ring.

"Same rules apply. If something happens to me, take the truck and get out of here." He left the keys in the ignition and shut the door gently, not wanting to wake the little boy. As he climbed the back porch steps, he noticed a soft glow coming from the kitchen and wondered if Ed had waited up for them. He peered inside, but there didn't seem to be anyone around.

Matt tapped softly on the door. Waited. When no one answered, he assumed his considerate hosts had left a lamp on so Matt and Jenna wouldn't have to enter a dark house.

He had just turned to retrieve the key from the planter box when a shot rang out across the property, and he instinctively dove for cover.

FIVE

Jenna sat straight up in her seat.

Was that a gunshot? She scanned the porch. But she didn't see Matthew.

He'd just been standing at the door, then turned…

And went down.

If something happens to me, take the truck and get out of here.

Jenna clicked into autopilot, climbed over the console and got behind the wheel of the truck. How on earth had they found them out here, in the middle of nowhere, at a safe house that no one knew about?

Adjusting the seat, she turned the ignition, shoved the truck in gear and hit the accelerator. Spinning the wheel, she whirled around and headed back out on the dirt trail, all the while waiting for another shot, for the shattering of glass. They'd no doubt shoot at her next, right?

Calm your breathing.

She kept her head low in anticipation of the next shot.

It never came.

As she distanced herself from the house, cautious hope tempered her panic.

The blink of the truck's headlights caught movement up ahead, but it wasn't a man waving a gun. A young woman in light blue pajamas was racing through the snow toward the main road. She wasn't wearing a jacket, and her feet were bare.

Jenna couldn't just drive by and do nothing. She lowered her window and called out to the girl. "What happened?"

The woman shrieked and stumbled, falling on the ground. Checking the rearview mirror for signs of danger, Jenna slowed to a stop and got out. She could do this quickly. She could save an innocent young woman.

Even if she'd been unable to save herself until it was too late.

She rushed to the woman, who was a teenager, she noticed as she got closer, one who was casting a worried glance over her shoulder.

"Come on, we've gotta go," Jenna said.

"Don't hurt me. Don't hurt me!" the girl cried, her eyes pinched shut.

"I'm here to help you."

And that's when she noticed the gun in her hand.

"Why do you have a gun?" Jenna automatically reached for it.

The teen scrambled away, clutching the gun with a deadly grip. She didn't aim it at Jenna—not yet anyway.

"It's okay," Jenna said.

"I saw him—he's here! He's never going to let me go!"

"Who, honey? Who's after you?"

"That's why I fired the gun, to warn him to stay away."

"Good, you did good," she encouraged.

If this young woman had fired the weapon, it meant the immediate danger had nothing to do with Billings's men who were after Jenna and Eli.

"I won't go back, I won't," she said with a wild look in her eyes.

She seemed irrational, crazed. Jenna wondered if she'd had a traumatic nightmare that drove her out into the night. Jenna had experienced plenty of those.

"I'm Jenna. What's your name?"

The young woman's eyes darted from Jenna to the truck to the surrounding property.

"Please? What's your name?" Jenna tried again.

"Emily."

"I'd really like to help you, Emily."

"No one can help me."

"That's what I used to think. I was married to a very bad man."

Emily blinked her tear-filled eyes at Jenna.

"Come on, it's cold out here, and you're barefoot." Jenna took a step toward her.

Emily scrambled to her feet and aimed the gun at Jenna.

Her heart pounding, Jenna put out her hand. "Please put down the gun. I suspect you had a nightmare that triggered bad memories."

"It was so real!"

"I know. I've had them too."

The wail of a child drifted from the open truck door. Eli had awakened, probably hungry with a wet diaper. Jenna strategized how to protect the child from a hysterical woman with a gun.

"That's…that's a baby," Emily said, lowering the weapon.

"Yes, a little boy named Eli."

"I had a baby," Emily said.

"Babies are wonderful."

Emily dropped the gun and fell to her knees. She buried her face in her hands. "I didn't mean it. I didn't mean it," she sobbed.

The sound of a car engine roared in the distance. Help was on the way.

Jenna couldn't wait. She couldn't risk Emily reaching for the gun again. She trudged through the snow, picked up the gun and tossed it out of reach. Emily didn't even notice. She was rocking back and forth, apologizing. Jenna suspected Emily had lost her child, just as Jenna had lost baby Joey.

It was surreal to be caught between the traumatized, crying young woman that reminded Jenna so much of herself, and baby Eli crying from the truck.

Jenna crouched beside Emily. "You're going to be okay."

"It was so real." Emily looked up, her face wet with tears. "I was so scared."

"I know." Jenna wrapped her arms around Emily. That's the only thing that had worked for Jenna when she stayed with Patrice, the only thing that quelled the terror. "He's not here now. And baby Eli needs us."

A car door slammed, then a second door.

"Jenna?" Matt said in a strained voice.

She glanced up at his worried expression. An older gentleman stood next to him. She assumed it was Ed Miller.

"We're okay," Jenna said.

"Eli…?" Matt glanced at the truck.

"He's fine. We're all fine."

"I'm sorry. I'm so sorry," Emily whimpered.

"Let's get back to the house," Matt said.

He took a step toward Jenna and Emily. Emily cowered, still clinging to Jenna.

"I'll ride back with Emily," Jenna said.

Matt hesitated, as if he were going to argue with her.

"Can you take care of Eli?" Jenna asked.

"Of course."

"She had a gun. I tossed it over there." Jenna pointed toward the field.

"I'll find it," Matt said.

"I don't understand what's going on here," Ed said.

"Please forgive me. I'm so sorry." Emily's muffled voice repeated the apology over and over.

"I'll explain everything back at the house." Jenna helped Emily stand. As they headed to Ed's truck, Matthew stopped her by placing a gentle hand on Jenna's shoulder. He didn't speak, but she read the relief in his eyes.

"I know," she said and offered a slight smile.

An hour later baby Eli was fast asleep in a downstairs guest room that he and Jenna shared. Matt had changed him, made him a bottle and soothed the child into a deep slumber, all while denying the intense emotions that ripped through him like a tornado over the Great Plains. It wasn't only the fear of breaking his promise to protect Jenna that threw him into utter panic, but something else, something he didn't want to consider.

He was developing feelings for Jenna North. Inappropriate feelings. What else could explain the tightness in his chest when he and Ed had pulled up behind his truck and he noticed the open door? For a second he thought Billings's men had found her and violently ripped her from behind the wheel of the truck.

Thankfully, Ed saw movement in the snow about fifty feet away.

It was Jenna, on the ground, comforting someone. A young woman who'd apparently broken into Ed's lockbox and taken a gun.

As Matt shut the door to the downstairs guest room where little Eli slept, he reconsidered his decision to stay in the same house as the young woman. The Millers had convinced him it would be safe because they'd called a counselor and off-duty cop to keep watch over the girl during the night. They couldn't move her from the house in the middle of the night, nor had they made the decision yet to do so.

Matt joined Jenna, Ed and Nancy, who had settled around the kitchen table to decompress. Nancy brewed tea and put out a tray of fresh fruit and banana bread.

"How about a moment of thanks that no one was hurt," Nancy suggested.

Matt bowed his head.

"Lord, thank you for watching over us tonight," Nancy began. "For protecting us from harm, and helping Emily find comfort in Jenna's kindness. Amen."

A unanimous *amen* filled the kitchen. Matt

thought he heard Jenna whisper a soft response but couldn't be sure.

"Well that was more excitement than I'm used to." Nancy slid the plate of fruit and bread toward Jenna. "And we've had our share of challenges with the girls."

"Why did she discharge the weapon?" Ed asked.

"It was a warning shot," Jenna explained.

"Warning who?"

"The man she thought was after her."

Ed shook his head.

"Those nightmares can seem very, very real," Jenna defended.

Matt wondered what kind of new nightmares would plague Jenna thanks to tonight's violence.

"Jenna," he said, "how are you doin'?"

She tipped her chin as if considering her answer. "Good. I'm okay. A little cold from being outside in the snow, I guess." She turned to Nancy. "Thanks again for letting us stay here tonight."

"You may stay as long as necessary." Nancy warmed Jenna's tea.

Jenna wrapped her hands around the teacup. "What will happen to Emily?"

"We'll have a meeting and discuss the best option," Ed said. "Our mission is to provide a safe environment for young women in trouble. What Emily did tonight, stealing one of my weapons..."

He hesitated. "It goes against the principles of our farm. I'm not sure she can remain here."

"That's so sad," Jenna said in a soft voice. "I mean, it's her abuser's fault she has nightmares."

"It depends on the counselors' evaluations," Nancy offered.

"Counselors, plural?" Jenna said.

"Behavioral counselor and chemical dependency counselor," Nancy said.

"Some girls have had their share of issues with drugs before coming to the farm," Ed explained. "We understand that, but they must be on the road to getting clean, and we have our boundaries. It's the best way to provide a safe environment."

"How long do they usually stay?" Jenna asked.

As Ed and Nancy discussed the inspiration behind their safe haven, and its rules, with Jenna, Matt worried that the details might be too painful for her, sparking violent memories of her past.

Yet she'd sounded sincere, even confident, a moment ago when she'd said she was okay.

He leaned back in his chair and took a calming breath. Only now did his pulse seem to slow to a normal rate.

After the gunshot earlier, Matt had quickly let himself in the house and found Ed and Nancy coming down the stairs in a panic.

At first Ed thought it was a neighbor warning off a bear, but then they discovered Emily was gone, and the firearm lockbox in the pantry had been broken into.

"They know the rules when they come here," Ed said. "Inappropriate behavior is not tolerated. And stealing one of my guns—"

"She was out of her mind and thought she needed to defend herself," Jenna said.

"Be that as it may, it's grand theft," Ed said.

"When she came out of her trauma, she kept apologizing and asking for your forgiveness. Isn't that what good Christians do? Forgive?"

"Jenna," Matt warned, questioning her tone.

"We do practice forgiveness, Jenna," Nancy interjected. "But we have to temper that with our goal of protecting our guests. If the counselors think her behavior is erratic to the point of being dangerous, we have to respect that evaluation and act accordingly."

"You can forgive someone and let them go," Matt said.

"How? How do you do that?" Jenna challenged.

"By realizing that all that anger and resentment you carry only serves to destroy you from the inside," Matt said, recalling his own anger with the driver who'd hit Sarah's car, causing it to slide into a tree, killing her upon impact.

Then again, if she hadn't been going twenty miles over the speed limit, she might still be alive. And she might still be alive if she and Matt hadn't argued, again, about his job being more important than their relationship. Maybe if he'd paid closer attention, maybe if…

No, he'd given up blaming himself and everyone else for her death.

"Forgiveness, well, it brings you out of the darkness," he said.

"Amen to that," Ed said.

Matt glanced at Jenna's puzzled look. He suspected he'd be interrogated about this conversation in the future, although he wasn't sure it was wise to share more details of his life, to cross even further over that line than he already had.

He was developing feelings for Jenna North. Time to put the brakes on before this thing between them spun out of control.

"We will certainly forgive Emily," Nancy said. "The bigger question is, will she be able to forgive herself?"

Nancy's words still haunted Jenna the next morning. *Will she be able to forgive herself?*

Jenna forced herself to stop thinking about self-forgiveness, frustrated by the resentment that particular thought conjured up. Instead, she focused on Eli. She'd thankfully awakened before the little boy, maybe because his sleep had been interrupted a few times last night, which caused him to sleep late.

She washed up and dressed in clothes Nancy

set aside for her, chosen from the wardrobe they kept for guests. The older woman had explained that most of the time, the young women came with nothing other than the clothes they wore when rescued.

Jenna could relate.

She headed for the kitchen to make Eli's morning bottle. As she passed by the living room, she noticed Matt was gone from the couch, the blanket neatly folded and draped over the back. He said he'd sleep better on the sofa than in a bed, but she wondered if he was actually positioning himself as the first line of defense.

I will protect you. An appreciative smile tugged at the corner of her lips.

The smell of coffee drew her into the kitchen, where she poured herself a cup, then warmed Eli's formula. There was enough for two, maybe three more bottles. They'd have to make a run to the store soon. As the bottle warmed, she leaned against the counter and noticed a high chair at the table. It seemed the Millers were prepared for anything.

The back door opened. Nancy came inside and kicked her boots on the mat. "Good morning."

"Morning. The coffee's amazing."

"I'm glad you like it. Ed got the high chair out of storage."

"I noticed. Thanks."

Nancy hung her jacket on the coatrack and stepped out of her boots and into clogs. "Eggs and toast for breakfast?"

"I'm not much of a breakfast person."

"Pancakes it is." She winked.

"Where is Matthew?"

"He and Ed are out doing chores."

Jenna was afraid to ask, but she had to know. "And Emily?"

"We're still debating. I see I guessed right about your size." Nancy scanned Jenna's sweatpants, T-shirt and fleece.

"Thanks, it's very comfortable."

"When you and Matt go to the store today, you can pick up more clothes, and supplies for the baby. Is he still asleep?"

"Yes. I want to be ready," Jenna said, shaking the warmed bottle.

"Smart girl."

Jenna felt such comfort, such support from Nancy. It reminded her of the Guardians, how she'd felt safe every step of her journey. That gave her an idea.

"Nancy, if you decide that Emily is too much of a risk, I might have an alternative for her."

Nancy glanced up from mixing the pancake batter.

"I know of a group that helps women get away

from violent situations. They might consider working with Emily."

"You have such a good heart, Jenna. So generous."

Warmth flushed Jenna's cheeks. She wasn't used to being praised.

The cry of a baby echoed through the house. "That's my cue," Jenna said.

"Bring him into the kitchen. My grandchildren loved my blueberry pancakes when they were his age."

"Sounds good."

By the time Jenna got to the bedroom, Eli was standing in the crib, gripping the top rail, tears streaming down his face.

"Hey, buddy, no need to cry." She noticed that he'd dropped his polar bear on the floor. "Look, it's Bubba." He rubbed it against his cheek and the cry turned into a whimper.

"Okay, hungry boy." Jenna offered the bottle, which he took with a firm one-handed grip. She carried him to the dresser that doubled as a changing table, complete with a soft pad and four-inch lip around the edges so he wouldn't roll off. Jenna absently started humming. Eli's eyes rounded with fascination at the sound.

It was strange, how she naturally changed his diaper, how she always seemed to know what would calm him. Yet it made sense, because she'd spent months preparing for her own child's arrival.

Thank you, Joey. Because of you, I'm able to take care of Eli.

The thought sparked warmth in her chest that melted a little of the cold, hard grief.

Once dressed, she carried Eli toward the kitchen, glancing upstairs and wondering how Emily was doing today. Jenna would call Patrice to inquire about the Guardians helping the young woman, but she'd have to tell them everything, including that Emily's trauma had resulted in a night terror that caused her to steal a gun.

"That might be a deal breaker," Jenna whispered to herself.

She and Eli entered the kitchen just as Matthew and Ed came in through the back door.

"Good morning," Jenna said, relieved to see him.

"Morning." Matthew took off his jacket and hung it on the rack.

"Any word from Marcus?" Jenna asked.

"No," Matthew answered.

"How'd the little dude sleep?" Ed reached out to squeeze Eli's foot.

Eli buried his face against Jenna's shoulder, still sucking on the bottle and clinging to his bear.

"Oh, he's playing shy, is he?" Nancy teased.

"He's certainly taken to you." Ed nodded at Jenna.

"Yeah, I guess he has," Jenna said, lightly kissing his head.

"Pancakes will be ready in a few minutes," Nancy said.

Jenna shifted Eli into the high chair and adjusted the tray in place. She glanced up and caught Matthew watching her.

"What, am I doing it wrong?" she asked.

"No, ma'am, quite the contrary."

She turned to Eli, wanting to avoid an awkward moment, another compliment that would make her blush bright pink.

"You two were out awhile," Nancy said to the men. "Didn't think picking stalls would take that long."

"Had some catching up to do," Ed said. "Although he couldn't explain why Jenna threw my gun into the snow last night."

Jenna shrugged. "Guns aren't my thing."

"Boo!" Eli dropped his polar bear. Matthew picked it up and put it back on his tray. Eli dropped it again.

"Ah, we're playing that game, are we?" Matthew said with a smile.

It all felt so surreal, sitting in this bright yellow kitchen with a little boy in a high chair, surrounded by such lovely people.

She enjoyed watching Matthew play with Eli, as if the federal agent hadn't a care in the world other than making the child giggle.

"I wonder if Tim and Miss Westbrook will stay for breakfast," Nancy said.

"Tim and Miss Westbrook?" Jenna said.

"The off-duty police officer and the counselor," Nancy said. "They're still upstairs."

"That reminds me, I want to call the people I mentioned last night, in case Emily can't stay here," Jenna said. "Could I use your phone?"

"Sure." Ed grabbed the cordless phone off the cradle and handed it to her.

"Can you watch Eli for a minute?" she asked Matt.

"Of course."

Jenna went into the living room to make the call. At this point she trusted the three people in the kitchen, but still felt protective of the Guardians.

"Hello?"

"Patrice, it's Jenna."

"I was hoping you'd call. How are you?"

"I'm good, at least for the time being."

"I'm so relieved you're okay."

"Thanks. I had great support last night." Jenna told Patrice about the Millers and their mission of helping women in trouble. She described Emily's violent reaction after being plagued by the nightmare.

"Makes sense," Patrice said. "She was reliving the horror."

"The thing is—" Jenna hesitated "—she stole a

gun from the couple here, and they might not be able to let her stay, especially if they have more guests arriving in the next few days. I don't suppose...?"

"You want me to ask the Guardians if they can help?"

"Would you?"

"I'd be happy to."

"Thank you so much. I'll get the number of the farm and you can speak with Nancy. I—" Jenna hesitated "—I don't know where we're going next or what kind of danger awaits us."

"Do you want to come stay at my place?"

Jenna couldn't rely on the Guardians forever. She needed to take care of herself at some point. "Thanks for the offer, but I'm with an FBI agent who is committed to helping me."

"And you trust him?"

"I'm working on it."

"I have faith in you."

Jenna wished she had that kind of faith in herself.

"I need to get Nancy's phone number. Hang on." Jenna went back into the kitchen and asked the Millers for the number of their landline.

"Better yet, let me speak with her." Nancy motioned for Ed to take over pancake duty.

"I'll go see if Tim and Miss Westbrook are staying for breakfast." Ed made a quick escape.

"It's just pancakes," Nancy called out with a

smile, then turned to Jenna. "He's afraid we'll be eating hockey pucks for breakfast."

"I'll take over." Matt stood and went to flip pancakes.

Jenna handed Nancy the phone and sat next to Eli to keep him entertained.

"Hi, this is Nancy." Nancy went into the living room, leaving Jenna and Matthew alone with the little boy.

"You can cook?" Jenna said.

Matt glanced over his shoulder. "Got to. I'm single and can't stand fast food."

"That's rare—I mean a bachelor not liking fast food."

"Don't get me wrong. I like an occasional pizza or a burger. I guess I'm kind of a health nut though. The cheap and greasy fast food can be a killer." He hesitated before flipping the pancakes. "Sorry."

He was apologizing for mentioning death by junk food, as anyone might in a normal conversation.

"You *will* be sorry if you don't get this guy a pancake pretty soon," Jenna said to lighten the mood. "He's almost done with his milk."

"We'll hit the store this morning before we leave town," Matt said. "He probably needs more formula, and I could use some clothes."

"We're not staying, even for one more night, are we?"

"Do you like it here?"

"Yeah. It feels normal, maybe even…safe."

Matthew chuckled as he turned to her. "You're the only civilian I know who gets threatened by a crazed woman with a gun in the middle of the night, and that feels safe."

"You know what I mean. The other parts, the Millers, this." She motioned to him, then reached out and stroked Eli's arm.

"It does, doesn't it?" he said softly. "Feel normal."

She couldn't rip her gaze away from his intense blue eyes. Her heartbeat sped up. What was happening here?

"May I ask you something?" he said cautiously.

"Sure."

"Aren't you worried about your ex-husband coming after you?"

The mention of her abuser shattered the tender moment.

"No, the group that helped me escape did a good job of covering my tracks."

"But guys like that don't tend to give up."

"He's in jail," she said. "After he put me in the hospital, I decided to press charges. Besides, my friend made me learn how to shoot."

"Yet you threw my firearm into the snow at the truck stop and tossed Ed's gun last night."

"I know how to handle a gun, but I don't relish the thought of shooting someone."

A few moments of silence passed, then he said, "I hope you never have to."

There he was, that gentle man again, offering comfort and compassion.

It made her uneasy.

"Bah!" Eli tossed his bear and it slid across the kitchen table.

"Someone's getting restless," she said, thankful for the interruption. She didn't like talking about Anthony, or the deal she'd agreed to in order to extricate herself from his life.

Matt flipped the pancakes. "I'd better make another pot of coffee too."

"Can I help?"

"Nope, I'm good."

Yes, he certainly was, she mused as she watched this broad-shouldered man move around the kitchen with ease.

But this pleasant scenario wasn't real, and she didn't know Matthew well enough to conclude he was a good man.

As he went to work on the coffee, she took a long, deep breath and enjoyed the scene a moment longer: a kind man cooking breakfast for Jenna and a child. She closed her eyes briefly, and the sweet smells and comforting sounds of a loving kitchen filled her senses with peace.

The coffee maker ground the beans, shattering the moment with a memory she thought she'd buried years ago.

Anthony's irrational rage and hateful words.

Fresh coffee—what does it take to make a fresh pot of coffee?

He'd hurled the glass pot across the room. Jenna ducked. The pot crashed against the wall, shattering into pieces.

Get down on your knees and clean that up!

She turned toward the closet.

What are you doing!

I'm getting the broom.

Clean it up with your hands.

But, Anthony...

He came at her, eyes blazing fire—

"Jenna?"

She glanced at Matthew, who stood only a few inches away. He narrowed his eyes as if deciding what to say. He was an intuitive man, and he knew she'd just been someplace else.

That dark place.

"Two pancakes or three?" he said.

Good, he wasn't going to ask her to explain her sudden mood shift.

"Go ahead and put three on a plate and I'll share with Eli," she said.

"Sounds good." When he didn't immediately turn away, she refocused her attention on Eli.

The longer she and Matthew made eye contact, the more likely he'd ask questions about her past, and she'd eventually open up to him. Yet she didn't want to. Sharing too much information could be dangerous, on many levels.

Ed joined them in the kitchen. "You made fresh coffee. Thanks."

"So, a couple dozen pancakes?" Matt said.

"Yep, I think I convinced them to stay for breakfast."

"Is Emily still asleep?" Jenna asked.

"Just woke up. She kept apologizing, begging me to let her stay. Poor kid."

Nancy came into the kitchen and hung up the phone. "What a nice lady," she said to Jenna.

"Patrice is the best."

"I think Gloria's Guardians could be a good option if Emily doesn't stay here."

Jenna cringed slightly at the use of the group's official name in front of Matthew, but he seemed to be conversing with Ed about how to make the perfect pancake.

"Ma!" Eli shouted, tapping his fingers to his lips.

"What a silly fellow," Nancy said.

"That's sign language for eat." Jenna had seen Chloe communicate with her son using basic sign language.

"Sign language? Isn't that something," Nancy said. "How long are you two staying?"

"I figured we'd leave after breakfast," Matthew said.

"Better yet, let us take care of Eli while you

shop for supplies. You certainly don't want a toddler underfoot while you're at the store."

Matthew slid a plate of pancakes in front of Jenna. "Are you comfortable with that?"

Putting her hands together in a hopeful pose, Nancy smiled at Jenna.

"The two of us would be less noticeable without Eli," Matt suggested.

"The little guy's safe here," Ed said. "And we don't have any guests coming for a couple of days."

"He'll take a midmorning nap while you're away," Nancy said. "That way he'll be refreshed for the next leg of your journey."

Jenna wasn't sure what to do. She'd promised Chloe she'd take care of Eli, and she'd done a good job so far. Could she risk leaving him at the farm for an hour or two?

"There is no wrong answer," Matthew said.

She glanced at Eli, who was savoring the pancakes he shoved into his mouth with his little hands. Who better to take care of him for a few hours than a grandmother who acted as a host for abused women?

The little boy might very well be on the run with Jenna and Matt for days, weeks even. Didn't he deserve a little normalcy?

Then she remembered Patrice's hope that someday Jenna would choose to make decisions from a place of love, not fear.

"We'll take him with us," Matt said.

"No." Jenna glanced into his blue eyes. "It's okay. He can stay with Nancy and Ed."

"Hallelujah," Nancy said, humming through the kitchen and pouring more batter onto the hot griddle.

Jenna smiled at little Eli, whose eyes widened with delight at biting into a juicy blueberry.

Matthew placed a gentle hand on Jenna's shoulder. Welcoming the gesture, she realized she was starting to feel comfort from his touch.

After breakfast they waited in the guest room for Emily, the counselor and the off-duty officer to leave. Matthew said the fewer people who knew that he, Jenna and Eli were at the Millers', the better.

Jenna settled herself on the floor to play with the little boy. Matthew joined them, pressing noise-making buttons on a fire truck, to Eli's delight. Once again, Jenna was lulled into the mirage of a happy family.

"Jenna?" Matthew said.

She looked at him.

"You okay?" he asked.

"Sure, why?"

"Your expression changed."

And he was way too intuitive. "I'm okay."

She grabbed a foam ball. "Eli, look!"

Eli spun around and she tossed him the ball. He

caught it and toddled across the room. He tripped on a block and tumbled forward.

Jenna dove to catch him, but was a second too late. He hit his head on the window ledge and started to whimper. "Ow-ee."

She hugged him and grabbed his bear. "You're okay, little boy. I'll fix the ow-ee." She kissed his forehead.

"Bubba's gonna give you a kiss too." Matthew nuzzled the boy's cheek with the bear, and whimpers quickly turned into giggles.

"Good save," she said.

He winked at her.

The echo of voices drifted through the door. Jenna tipped her head and could hear Emily's voice. She was crying, begging for forgiveness.

Jenna sighed and hoped Gloria's Guardians could help the young woman.

Eli suddenly wound up and tossed the foam ball at Matthew's face.

"Oh, yeah?" Matthew said in a silly voice.

The little boy charged. Matthew caught him and gave him a big hug.

"You ever think about having children?" Jenna asked.

"Nah, not with my hours."

What a shame, because he was a natural with Eli.

Nancy tapped on the door and cracked it open. "Everyone's gone. How's the little guy doing?"

"Back and forth between high octane and wanting a nap," Matthew said, standing up. "Why don't you two get going? Ed and I will take care of Eli's every need."

Half an hour later, Jenna and Matt were at the Super Store in town, picking out supplies. She felt so relieved that Eli hadn't put up a fuss when they'd left him behind. Of course it helped that Ed was playing Legos with the little boy, distracting him so she and Matthew could leave unnoticed. They decided to take Ed's truck as a precaution.

Jenna's goal was to purchase clothes, baby supplies and snacks. She wasn't stressed about Eli because she'd made the decision to leave him with the Millers from a place of love for the child, not fear of danger.

Once the cart was filled with baby items—formula, diapers, baby wipes, backup pacifiers and clothes—she found hair color and then went to the women's clothing section. She was especially excited to find the baby carrier Patrice had mentioned. It would allow Jenna to conveniently strap Eli to her body. Matthew stayed close, acting the role of supportive husband and doting dad.

"Blond, huh?" he said, analyzing the box of color while she sifted through a rack of shirts.

"What's wrong with blond?"

"Seems kind of harsh for such a pretty face."

She snapped her attention to him.

"Sorry, that just came out." He tossed the box into the cart and glanced at her. "You're blushing?"

"I've had three compliments today. A world record for me."

"You deserve more than three a day," he said with a slight smile.

She broke eye contact, unnerved by the tender moment. "You're trying to make me blush again."

"What's that about?" he said.

"I'm not used to getting compliments, so I blush." She furiously searched the rack. "It's embarrassing, but—"

Her words caught in her throat because he'd interlaced his fingers with hers. It was such an intimate connection. She glanced at his concerned expression.

"Come with me. Leave the cart," he said.

She followed his instruction, still processing the physical contact.

As he led her through the women's clothing section toward the back of the store, she studied the hard set to his jaw and his pursed lips.

"What's going on?" she said.

"I think they found us."

"*They* as in Billings's men?" She squeezed his hand for strength.

He squeezed back, but didn't look at her. Matthew led her through an employees-only door. Where was he taking her?

He pulled her into the stockroom, where rows of consumer goods were stacked high up to the ceiling.

"Matthew—"

"Shh." He guided her into a small alcove with boxes on either side of them. "I need you to trust me on this."

And he kissed her.

SIX

"Hey, what are you...? Uh, disgusting," someone said behind them.

Matt had seen a teenager turn the corner up ahead, eyeing his phone. Knowing the kid would be able to identify him and Jenna, Matt did the only thing he could think of.

He kissed Jenna North.

Breaking the kiss, he whispered, "Sorry," against her ear.

Matt held on to her as he listened intently to the sounds in the warehouse, waiting until he was sure the teen had passed by and they were safe.

Then again, would the kid run off and tell security he saw two customers necking in the stockroom?

"What...what just happened?" she said.

"I saw a security guard leading a cop in our direction. We needed to disappear."

"But you kissed me."

"A teenager was about to spot us."

Poking his head around the corner, Matt saw the cop and security guard walking in the opposite direction. Matt needed to get Jenna out of here. He handed her the truck keys, but she put up her hands to refuse them.

"Jenna, you haven't changed your hair color. You'll be easily recognizable. Take Ed's truck. Get to the farm. If I'm not back in an hour, take off."

"What are you going to do?"

"Distract them so you can get away."

"I'm not leaving."

He looked into her green eyes. "You are, and you know why?"

She shook her head.

"Because Eli needs you. I can take care of myself. Now go." He motioned to the dock where they unloaded goods.

With a reluctant sigh, she glanced both ways and took off toward the exit. As she approached the door, she shot him a quick glance before disappearing into the sunshine.

Sudden regret knotted in his gut. What if this cop was dirty and there were men waiting for her outside? Matt started to follow her.

"Stop right there," a male voice ordered.

Matt slowly turned around.

The store security guard and police officer approached him.

"I was looking for the bathroom, sorry," Matt said.

"Yeah, right," the security guard, who appeared to be in his midtwenties, said. The cop was older, but not by much.

"Are you alone?" the police officer said.

"Yes, sir." Because he was. At this moment anyway.

"Let's go." The cop, whose badge read Richter, pulled cuffs off his belt. The hair pricked on the back of Matt's neck. Really? Officer Richter was cuffing Matt for trespassing in the stock area?

"He's gotta be a part of the crew," the guard said.

"Crew?" Matt asked.

"Save it," the guard said. "You're done stealing from us."

What had Matt walked into?

"Come on." Richter motioned to him.

Matt didn't resist, not wanting to make a scene, and offered his wrists. The cop snapped the cuffs in place and led him through the store to the public exit. Heat rushed to Matt's cheeks at the shameful march past young mothers who held their children close, and employees taking pictures with smartphones.

Great. Now his face would be plastered all over

the internet, making him an easy target. Yep, it had been a good decision to separate from Jenna.

But was she safe?

Once outside, he glanced toward the spot where the truck had been parked. It was gone. He sighed with relief.

Then he scanned the lot and caught sight of it, the window down, Jenna watching as Matt was led to the cruiser. He shook his head slightly, warning her to keep her distance.

Officer Richter put Matt in the back seat and shut the door. He stood outside the car and called in on his shoulder radio. A good thing, since Matt could use a few minutes to strategize.

At first he'd thought this was related to the money-laundering case, but when the security guard accused Matt of stealing, he realized this was more likely a wrong-place, wrong-time situation. Talk about bad timing.

Didn't matter. He had to talk his way out of this and get back to Jenna.

He'd promised to protect her and Eli, and he would fulfill that promise.

He debated what and how much to tell Officer Richter. Should he admit he was FBI? Continue his role as Matthew the janitor? Maybe a little of both? If he told this police officer he was undercover, maybe he could enlist his help in fleeing the county.

Not likely. Billings would probably reach out

to cops statewide, making up some story about the janitor and the child kidnapper, Jenna North.

It had been a wise move to send Jenna away. Matt strained to look out the window. The truck was nowhere in sight.

Leaning back against the seat, Matt planned out his next steps. He'd tell Richter that he was undercover FBI, but couldn't share specifics of his case.

The door opened and Officer Richter got behind the wheel of the cruiser.

"Officer, I need to tell you something," Matt started.

"No, you don't. You have the right to remain silent..."

Jenna paced the Millers' kitchen, anxiously twirling her silver ring. She wrestled with panic that taunted her thoughts.

More than two hours had passed, and still no word from Matt.

"Jenna, please relax," Nancy said, sitting at the kitchen table.

"I'm trying," Jenna said, unable to stop her anxious pace.

Eli was still napping, and the bottle was warming for when he awakened. Ed had gone back to the Super Store, and Jenna had given him her emergency cash to purchase the items she'd left in the cart.

"It was a misunderstanding," Nancy said. "They'll figure it out."

"We should have heard something by now." Jenna stopped and looked at Nancy. "He told me to leave if he wasn't back in an hour but...but I can't bring myself to abandon him."

"You care about Matt," the woman said in a knowing voice.

The memory of their kiss made Jenna's lips tingle all over again. It had been years since she'd let a man kiss her.

Years since she actually enjoyed kissing a man back.

That hadn't been a real kiss, she reminded herself. It was a maneuver to keep them out of danger.

"He's a good man. I can see why you've fallen for him," Nancy said.

Jenna felt the need to correct her. "It's not like that. He's helped me so much. I owe it to him not to leave him behind."

"You may stay here as long as you like. However, we do have new guests coming in forty-eight hours, which means more people will know your whereabouts."

"True," Jenna said.

"Matt explained your situation, how people are looking for you and that law enforcement from Cedar River are involved in something nefarious."

"He told you what happened to Eli's mother?"

"Yes." Nancy patted the table. "Please, sit with me."

Jenna collapsed in a kitchen chair. Nancy put her hands together and whispered something under her breath. For once, Jenna wished she could join her in prayer, wished she knew the right words to ask for help, to beg for Matthew's safety.

"Amen," Nancy whispered and smiled at Jenna. "Do you pray, Jenna?"

"No."

"Why not?"

Jenna shrugged. A few seconds passed.

"Why do you pray?" Jenna asked.

"Because surrendering my worries to God gives me such peace. After all, God does not want us to worry."

"How do you know that?"

"In Philippians it reads, 'Be careful for nothing; but in every thing by prayer and supplication with thanksgiving let your requests be made known unto God.'"

The woman's faith was so pure, so sincere. If only Jenna could feel the same way about God—but He'd abandoned her far too many times for Jenna to have faith.

"Why are you afraid to pray?" Nancy asked.

"He'll just ignore me again."

"Are you sure He's been ignoring you? Maybe you didn't see the blessing."

"I lost my baby because of an abusive husband," Jenna said flatly.

"Oh, honey, I'm sorry." Nancy leaned over and gave her a hug.

A tear trailed down Jenna's cheek.

No, she couldn't afford to cry. Tears meant weakness.

Jenna broke the embrace and stood. "I'd better pack. When Ed gets home with the supplies, I had better leave. That's what Matthew would want me to do, to keep moving."

"How about I put together some food for you and Eli?" Nancy stood and went to gather supplies.

She didn't seem offended in the least that Jenna had brushed her off and shut down the conversation about God and prayer.

"That would be great, thanks," Jenna said. "I'll help."

Because she had to do something to keep busy until she left. The not knowing, the worrying about Matthew, was tearing her up inside.

Please, God...

She caught herself reaching out to the Lord and quickly pulled the thought back. Being around the Millers must be affecting her better judgment.

"Oh, here comes Ed," Nancy said, peering out the window. "And a police car. That's curious."

Jenna rushed to the window and spotted the Millers' truck, followed by a police car.

"I'll wait in Eli's room until you tell me it's safe." Jenna grabbed the bottle.

Nancy turned to her. "Oh, okay."

It must not have occurred to Nancy that the police car could be here for Jenna, that somehow Billings's men had found her.

She rushed into the guest room, and shut and locked the door. Heart racing, she scanned the room for options. Didn't make sense to climb out the window with Eli. She wouldn't get far in the snow.

If he can't find you, he can't hurt you.

Jenna scooped Eli out of the crib. The little boy fussed a little, but not much. She went into the oversize closet and shut the door. Eli started to squirm so she offered him the bottle.

She struggled to calm her frantic thoughts. What if this was it? What if the police were here to take Eli back to his father and arrest Jenna for kidnapping? Jenna scolded herself for not getting something in writing from Chloe about her wishes that Jenna be Eli's guardian. But Jenna hadn't sensed the danger was immediate, that she would, in fact, find herself Eli's guardian within minutes of her conversation with Chloe.

And here Jenna was, cornered again. Hiding. Terrified.

No, she counseled herself. Nancy and Ed would surely protect her and Eli.

They'd do their best, sure, but they wouldn't break the law. They were good people.

She was alone. With danger hovering in the next room.

"It's locked," a muted male voice echoed from the next room.

They were here. They were going to break into the bedroom and find her.

Hugging Eli, she whispered, "I won't let them hurt you."

Seconds stretched by. Then minutes. It felt like forever.

Three soft taps vibrated against the closet door. She bit back a soft gasp.

"Jenna?"

The closet door opened, and Matthew's silhouette hovered above her.

"What are you guys doin' in there?" he asked. "Playing hide-and-seek?"

Eli kicked his feet with delight.

"I thought… I wasn't sure…" was all Jenna could get out.

"It's safe. You can come out."

She didn't move, still processing his words.

"Here, I'll take Eli," he said.

She clung tighter to the child.

It's safe.

She knew better. It was never safe.

Her body started trembling uncontrollably, and

she wasn't sure why. It felt like her mind had shut down and the rest of her was in survival mode.

"You wanna know what happened after you left?" Matthew said, sitting on the floor beside the closet. "First, I was handcuffed and marched through the store like a criminal. I guess I can say I know how *that* feels now. Then the local cop starts to read me my rights, even though I'm trying to explain that I'm FBI. Figured that might earn me a get-out-of-jail-free card. He wasn't buying it. Apparently I fit the description of a guy they think is behind a theft ring at multiple retail stores. You know, tall, dark and handsome with a charming personality. What do you think? Does that pretty much describe me?"

Jenna glanced at him. Handsome? Yes, he was handsome.

He was also smiling. Smiling?

"Everything's...okay?" she said. He wouldn't be smiling if it weren't.

"It's all good."

"But...you were arrested?"

"Taken in for questioning. Eventually managed to convince the local police I'm FBI. It helped that Ed showed up to confirm my identity and that I've got history with Millers' farm. I explained that a case drew me to the Super Store and I was following someone when they found me in the back. Said I'm undercover and wanted to keep it that way, which is why I didn't reveal my identity to the security guard."

"They released you?"

"They did, and everything is A-okay."

They weren't coming to take Eli away.

They weren't going to lock Jenna up.

She took a breath. "I wasn't sure I'd ever see you again." It suddenly hit her how much she'd miss his company, his strength, maybe even… his faith.

"You know I'll always do my best to get to you," he said.

She nodded.

"I made you a promise, Jenna."

"Yes, you did."

"Come on out, sweetheart. It's all good, for now."

At first Matt didn't think he'd be able to coax her out of the closet. He recognized that look on her face. He'd seen it before, both on abused victims…

And on Jenna.

This remarkable woman, determined to protect her friend's child, still struggled with post-trauma issues.

Being thrown into this dangerous situation as Eli's guardian was definitely not helping. He wondered what would help.

She was out of the closet, but chose to stay in

the bedroom, while Matt joined the others in the kitchen. He could hardly blame her, considering Officer Richter's presence. The fewer people who knew her whereabouts, the better.

It had been Ed's idea to invite the cop to the farm as a gesture of thanks for contacting Matt's supervisor to confirm his identity instead of locking Matt in a cell.

As Ed and Nancy chatted with Officer Richter about town happenings, Matt excused himself to call his boss. He stepped out onto the front porch.

"Pragge," he answered.

"It's Weller. Thank you for clearing things up with the local PD."

"You're welcome. You on your way back to Cedar River?"

"Not yet, sir. I won't leave Jenna and the child until I'm confident they're safe."

"I'll send an agent right away."

Something told Matt that she wouldn't be safe with just any agent.

"We tried that before at the hospital, and one of Billings's men showed up."

"What are you insinuating?"

"I don't believe in coincidences, not where criminals are concerned."

"They were probably listening to the police scanner. You said a trooper escorted you to the hospital?"

"Yes, sir."

"Then that's how they knew."

"I'm not convinced."

"We need you back at the community center."

"Sir, instinct tells me the Jenna North situation is related to the money-laundering case. Give me a few days to prove it. I'll call my boss at the center and say I need a few days off."

Silence, then: "You've got forty-eight hours."

Pragge ended the call. Matt heard the inference behind the order—if he didn't return to his post in forty-eight hours, his career with the FBI would be in serious jeopardy, if not immediately over.

He rolled his neck and called Mrs. Harris at the community center, leaving a message that he had an emergency and needed to take some personal time.

Two days. He had two days to figure this out.

He went back into the house and joined Ed, Nancy and Officer Richter in the kitchen.

"Want a warm-up, Matt?" Nancy started to get up from the kitchen table.

"I've got it, thanks." Matt refreshed his mug of coffee.

"Officer Richter joined our local police department six months ago from…?" Nancy glanced at the cop.

"Seattle," Richter answered.

"How are you liking it so far?" Ed asked.

"A lot more snow than I'm used to."

"Yes, but not as much rain," Ed offered.

"I don't mind the rain." Officer Richter turned to Matt. "How long have you been with the FBI?"

"Ten years."

"Your supervisor sounds like a tough guy."

"He's feeling a lot of pressure to close a case."

The cop finished his coffee and placed his mug in the sink. "Well, let me know if there's anything I can do to help." He handed Matt a business card. "Sorry about bringing you in."

"You were doing your job." Matt tucked the guy's card in his shirt pocket.

"Ed, Nancy, thanks for the coffee." With a polite nod, Officer Richter left.

"Such a nice young man," Nancy said.

Matt went to the window and watched him pull away. "I'd better pack up. Ed—" he turned "—what do I owe you for the supplies?"

"Nothing. Jenna gave me a bunch of cash. Here's the change."

Matt took the money. Old habits die hard, he thought. He assumed she kept a wad of cash handy in case she needed to make a quick escape.

"I wish you could stay a few days," Nancy said. "We love having Eli, and I think Jenna could use a little TLP."

"You mean TLC?" Matt said.

"No, I mean TLP. Tender loving prayer." Nancy winked.

"That she could, but it's better if we keep moving. You may like Officer Richter, but he might innocently mention my presence to a coworker and word could spread. I'm not sure who to trust."

"Even on the police force?" Ed said.

"Even on the force."

"Okay, well, I'll bring the shopping bags in from the truck." Ed grabbed his coat off the rack.

"And I'll organize them for you," Nancy offered.

"I can't thank you guys enough," Matt said.

Going back to the guest room, Matt hoped and prayed that Jenna was okay. A cold chill had rushed through him earlier when he'd opened the door to an empty room. The thought that she'd been taken…

But she hadn't been kidnapped. She was huddled in the closet, clutching the little boy in her arms. Matt fought the urge to kneel down and pull her into his arms, to hold her until she no longer trembled with fear.

He knew Jenna had to come out of her traumatic moment on her own, by her own will and strength. That was the best way for someone with an emotional wound like that to heal.

And that's what he wanted for the lovely Jenna North—he wanted her to heal and be at peace.

To feel safe.

The only way to accomplish that was to stay with her and protect her, because he wouldn't abandon someone he cared about.

He…cared about her?

You're never here. Your job is more important than our relationship.

Sarah's words taunted him, reminding him how he'd failed, and how that failure led to her senseless death. He'd prayed to God to forgive him for not being there for Sarah, for not making her a priority. He wouldn't make that mistake again.

Jenna would not die because Matt was distracted by his job. Somehow he had to protect Jenna *and* satisfy his boss. Time to take the offense and determine a connection between the money-laundering case and Chloe McFadden's murder, because his gut was screaming that they were connected.

He tapped on the bedroom door. "It's Matt."

"Come in," she called.

He opened the door and hesitated, appreciating the sight before him. Jenna sat on the floor helping Eli make a tower of wooden blocks. Matt's heart warmed.

Would he ever come home to this sight? Would he be able to find balance in his life, to draw the boundary that would allow him to be a good agent and also have a family?

"Look what Eli made," she said.

The little boy grinned, a twinkle in his eye. What a resilient kid. With a firm grip on his white polar bear, he swung at the tower of blocks and they crashed to the floor.

He dove at Jenna and she caught him in her arms. "What a silly boy."

She tickled his ribs, and he giggled through the pacifier clutched between his teeth. Rocking the little boy with ease, she glanced at Matt.

Oh, she'd recovered all right. It seemed that she, too, was resilient.

"Is the police officer gone?" she asked.

"He is."

"I'm glad your supervisor vouched for you."

"He did, but I got an earful."

"About?"

"He's cranky that I'm not back at the community center sweeping floors."

"Oh, right." She hesitated. "Your crucial undercover assignment."

"Protecting you is just as crucial, Jenna. Come on, we'd better get going."

"Do I have time to change my hair color?"

"How long do you need?"

"Probably an hour."

"That'll work. Will give me time to do a little digging. Ed has offered to swap trucks temporarily."

"Sounds good. You think Nancy can watch Eli while I do my hair?"

"I think she'd be offended if you didn't ask. She's going to miss him when we leave."

Jenna nuzzled Eli's hair. "Hear that? Everyone loves you."

She was right. And Matt topped that list. Who wouldn't love a sweet little boy with an infectious giggle and full-cheeked grin?

Matt's phone vibrated and he glanced at the screen. "Blocked number," he said.

"Maybe it's Marcus."

He didn't miss the hope in her voice. "Hello?" Matt answered.

"Is Jenna there?"

"Who's calling?"

"Marcus, Chloe's cousin."

"Hang on." Matthew handed her the phone.

"Hello?… Yes, oh, thank you so much for calling back. Chloe gave me your contact information… I'd rather not say over the phone, but Chloe was confident that you could help us."

Matthew fisted his hand, not wanting to pass off Jenna and Eli to a stranger.

"What's the address?… Sure, text it to this number," she said into the phone. "I'm not sure, maybe a few hours. I must warn you, it's dangerous."

Then she actually smiled.

"Oh, that's good to know. Thanks." With a sigh, she handed Matt the phone.

"You look happy," he said.

"I can see why Chloe wanted me to find Marcus. He's a former Navy SEAL who works in private security. His cabin is a little over three hours away. He gave me the access code and said he'd meet us later."

"He's not there?"

"No, he's on his way back from a job. He'll arrive tonight. His neighbor plows the drive for him when he's out of town so he said we should be fine."

"I'll do a background check on Marcus, just to be safe."

"Hopefully by tomorrow you'll be able to hand me off and focus on your real job."

He nodded in response. He should be pleased with the development. Instead, a flash of dread ripped through him. Would he really be able to leave the fragile Jenna North in the hands of a stranger?

While Matt waited at the kitchen table for Jenna, he called his good friend Agent Bob Barnes at the Bureau to do the background check on Marcus. Matt trusted Bob probably even more than his own boss at this point.

"What's got Pragge all worked up?" Bob asked.

"I called an audible."

"And you need me to catch the pass?"

"Something like that. Can you do a background check on Marcus Garcia, former Navy SEAL?"

"Sure, no problem. What about your current assignment?"

"This is related to the money-laundering case."

"Then why is Pragge snapping everyone's heads off?"

"I haven't convinced him of the connection yet. I might need your help with that too."

"You're gonna owe me."

"All-you-can-eat pizza at Marietti's?" Matt offered.

"Deal. I'll get working on this."

"Thanks, man, appreciate it."

"You're welcome. Be careful."

Matt studied his phone, hoping he'd made the right decision, that he hadn't exposed himself and Jenna to more danger by involving Bob. But Matt trusted Bob, especially after everything he'd done to support Matt after Sarah's death.

Bob had listened to and challenged Matt about his self-blame.

You didn't put her in the car. You didn't speed through town during a snowstorm.

No, but their argument had caused Sarah to tear off, wanting to get away from Matt as quickly as possible.

"Hey," Jenna said.

Matt noticed her standing in the doorway, but didn't respond right away. His mind was stuck in the past.

"That bad, huh?" She fingered her blond hair.

"No, sorry. I was distracted. It looks good."

"Thanks, but I know it's kinda harsh."

"Not harsh. Different, but you could never look harsh."

A smile tugged at the corner of her lips, and she glanced at the floor. Pink crept up her cheeks.

She looked adorable.

That's when it hit Matt that handing her off to a Navy SEAL who didn't have an emotional connection to Jenna might be the best way to keep her safe, because if Matt didn't watch it, the line between protector and love interest might not only blur, but could disappear completely.

How was that possible? After Sarah's death he'd made himself a promise not to get emotionally involved until he took a less demanding role with the agency.

"You okay?" She studied him as if trying to read his mind.

"Sure, we're packed and ready to go."

Matthew seemed oddly quiet during the drive to Marcus's cabin. At first Jenna thought he might be concerned about the intense snow falling across the Montana countryside, but then she sensed it was something else. His silence worried her.

"Did you find out anything about the case? Or about Marcus?" she asked.

"Marcus is clean."

"Oh, that's a relief. What about the case?"

"Nothing new. I'm limited as to how much I can do remotely."

She wondered if he regretted leaving his post at the community center to protect Jenna and Eli.

"Well, it won't be for much longer," she said. "Once we find Marcus, you can get back to Cedar River."

He didn't answer, not even a nod or grunt.

Then she had another thought: maybe he didn't like the idea of abandoning her and Eli. Had he felt the same tug of intimacy toward her that she'd been feeling over the past twenty-four hours? She tried telling herself it was normal to feel so close to someone this quickly considering the circumstances. Patrice thought Jenna had been growing dependent on the attorney who took her case against Anthony, and she'd cautioned Jenna. But what she felt for the lawyer had been pure gratitude. She couldn't thank him enough for doing the work pro bono and extricating her from the abusive marriage.

The way she felt about Matthew seemed different, which didn't mean it was any more real than what she'd felt for her attorney. It was another form of gratitude, that's all.

Then why did his opinion of her blond hair matter so much?

Forget it, Jenna. This is not a real relationship.

In truth, she'd noticed Matthew the janitor months ago, noticed his kind demeanor, his natural way with kids when he told them to slow down as they raced through the community center.

"Where did you get that?"

His question startled her.

"I'm sorry?"

He nodded at the braided silver ring she twirled on her right hand. "You tend to play with your ring when you're thinking."

She eyed the piece of jewelry. "Patrice from Gloria's Guardians gave it to me."

He already knew the name of the group, so she didn't feel the need to keep it a secret any longer.

"The ring is a reminder that we're all connected, and they're always there for me, that God's always there," she said. "I wish I could believe that."

"Why can't you?"

She shook her head, feeling herself being pulled down that dark path.

"Look at the positive ways God has touched your life," Matthew said. "The women who helped you escape your abusive husband, and the fact you've been able to keep Eli safe. You've been through trauma in your marriage, but that trauma gave you strength to take care of little Eli."

"I suppose, but I just can't believe in God."

"You don't have to," he said. "God's always there, whether you believe in Him or not."

No, this was definitely not someone she could

grow more attached to, not with his strength of faith. She glanced out the passenger window.

"I didn't mean to upset you," he said.

"You didn't." She turned to check on Eli, who slept peacefully in the back.

"He's blessed to have you in his life."

She snapped her attention to him. "I wouldn't say that."

"I would." He glanced at her.

Jenna's heartbeat sped up. She ripped her gaze from Matthew's assessing eyes and looked out the front window. In the distance she saw a small cabin, lit with a soft glow.

"That must be it," she said, thankful they were close.

"The lights are on. Maybe he beat us there."

"Actually, he said he'd turn the lights on remotely from his phone."

Matthew drove down the long, narrow driveway, somewhat plowed and bordered by a four-foot wall of snow on either side. "I'll leave the keys just in case."

"No," she said.

"Excuse me?"

"We're stronger together, Matt. Besides, it'll be safe. No one knows we're here except for Marcus."

"Perhaps, but I'm leaving the keys, for my peace of mind."

Matt continued around to the back of the property and parked next to three cars.

"He said he collected cars," she offered.

"Wait here."

He grabbed his gun from the glove box. Leaving the keys in the ignition, he got out of the truck and headed around to the front of the house.

When Matthew disappeared out of sight, Jenna turned her attention to Eli, who stirred behind her.

"Hey, little one. You awake?"

She climbed into the back seat and stroked his cheek, still thinking about Matthew's words, that Eli was blessed to have Jenna in his life.

Eli opened his eyes and kicked his feet, motioning to his mouth to indicate that he was hungry. She pulled a pack of fruit snacks out, something to keep him happy until they got inside. She wondered what was taking so long.

She glanced at the cabin. Through the falling snow she spotted Matthew stumbling around the corner motioning wildly.

Before she could comprehend what was happening, a man rushed Matthew from behind and tackled him.

SEVEN

They'd found her. How was that possible?

Jenna froze, unable to think, paralyzing fear shooting across her body to her fingertips.

She thought she'd conquered the fear after she'd left Anthony and relocated safely to Cedar River. If that were the case, she'd be taking the offensive right now instead of cowering in the back seat with a child who needed her protection.

Eli burst into wails, breaking the spell.

She climbed into the front seat and gripped the steering wheel with trembling hands.

"I can do this." She shoved the truck into gear and hit the gas. The back wheels spun, digging into the snow. The last thing she wanted was to get stuck.

She needed to calm down.

She didn't dare glance up again, didn't want the distraction. Matthew would tell her to put Eli first, to flee, escape.

Taking a deep breath, she touched the gas

pedal, more gently this time. Anthony rarely let her drive, always criticizing her for not signaling properly or for riding the brake.

What, are you stupid?

"No, Anthony, I'm not stupid," she ground out.

Clenching her jaw, she grew even more determined and pulled away. When the wheels started to lose their grip she eased up on the gas.

The truck was moving, slowly, but it was moving. Once she felt the wheels grip the snow, she increased pressure on the accelerator, eyes locked on the main road in the distance. Snow started blowing sideways, the storm intensifying, making it a challenge to see. She flicked on the wipers.

A gunshot echoed across the property.

She shrieked, instinctively ducked and picked up speed.

She was done being afraid. Always on edge.

She was a fighter.

Faster, she had to go faster.

Another gunshot rang out. The truck jerked left. The bullet must have hit her back tire.

She struggled to regain control. Gripped the wheel. How far could she drive with a flat tire?

Please, God, help me.

She'd do what was necessary to protect Eli, what she hadn't been able to do for Joey.

A third shot pierced the night air.

She jerked the wheel. Left, right. She had to get control.

The truck jettisoned forward into a snowbank. The momentum snapped her forward, and her head banged against the steering wheel.

Stars flashed across her vision.

Matt pulled on the metal handcuffs binding his wrists, his arms wrapped around a wooden support beam. His attacker had gotten Matt in a choke hold, applied enough pressure to make Matt pass out, then dragged him in here.

The guy only got the advantage because Matt needed to warn Jenna about the danger—the assailant who'd jumped Matt inside the cabin.

All was eerily quiet outside. Jenna had to have gotten away, right? Or else the guy had found her and Eli, taken them…

He pulled violently on the cuffs, panic eating away at his insides. He almost lost it, and he cried out to God, begging for help.

No, she'd be okay. She had to be. He wouldn't accept the alternative. Although still traumatized by her past, Jenna was a strong woman determined to save the little boy's life.

Nothing would stop her.

Matt scanned the room for a way to free himself. Who was this guy anyway? He must be working for Billings, although why not send the two men who'd assaulted Matt at the truck stop?

Bigger question: How had Jenna and Matt been tracked to Marcus's place?

No one knew they were coming here except for Marcus, and his background check had come up clean.

Agent Bob Barnes confirmed that Marcus was a decorated former SEAL who'd gone into private security work.

A gunshot rang out in the distance.

Then the wail of a car horn.

"No." He pulled more vehemently on his cuffs, panic, rage and desperation rushing his body.

He had to get it together, had to calm down so he could think.

Minutes ticked by slowly, painfully, as his imagination sucked him into the dark place, a familiar place.

Unable to stop her, to save her.

Hearing how they'd had to cut her out of the crumpled car.

Her dead body.

Guilt sliced through him. His fault; it had been his fault. Just like whatever was happening to Jenna out there was also his fault.

He yanked on the cuffs, the metal scraping his skin, his wrists starting to bleed. Intellectually he knew this was not helping, but his panic was stronger than his intellect.

A passage in the Bible came to mind—*Casting all your care upon Him; for He careth for you.*

It was worth a try. Repeating the verse from the Book of Peter, Matt took a deep breath and closed his eyes, forgiving himself for allowing the current situation to get so out of control. Forgiving himself for losing his advantage…

For the fact that he might lose Jenna.

No, he wouldn't allow that thought to torture him.

Repeating the Bible verse over and over, he continued to scan the room for something to use on the handcuffs.

The cabin door opened.

His attacker entered the cabin, carrying a crying Eli in the car seat.

"Where's Jenna?" Matt demanded.

Without a word, the guy placed the car seat by the sofa and went back outside.

She had to still be alive.

He wasn't sure he could survive the alternative.

Eli started wailing and kicking his feet.

"Hey, Eli," Matt said.

His little arms punched the air. The boy wanted out of his car seat, probably needed a diaper change and he was no doubt hungry too.

"It'll be okay, buddy," he offered. Matt remembered how Jenna had sung to him in the truck. He softly sang a favorite country ballad, and the little boy's eyes widened at the sound of Matt's deep voice. What Eli really needed was his pacifier, his little white bear.

A hug from Jenna.

A few minutes later the door opened again, and the bearded guy stormed inside.

Carrying Jenna over his shoulder.

Matt automatically fisted his hands. "What happened?"

The assailant dropped Jenna on the sofa and went to look out the window. Even from here, Matt could tell the snowfall had turned into a blizzard.

"Is she okay?" Matt demanded. He couldn't see her well enough to determine her injuries, but thought he saw a smudge of blood on her cheek. "Well, is she?"

"She's unconscious."

"But is she okay?"

"How would I know?" the assailant shouted and glared at Matt. "I'm not a doctor."

Upset by the guy's tone of voice, Eli burst into another round of wails.

The guy snapped his attention to the little boy. With narrowed eyes and a firm set to his lips, he took a step closer to Eli.

"I can calm him down," Matt offered.

The man took another step toward Eli.

"Try giving him the Binky," Matt said.

"I don't do kids."

"I practically raised my nephew. They call me the baby whisperer."

The guy glanced from Matt to Eli, considering.

"Look, you've got the gun," Matt said.

"That's right, I do." The assailant slowly turned and went to the sofa. Hovering over Jenna's unconscious body, he pressed the gun barrel against her head. "I would have no problem pulling the trigger on this one."

Matt fisted his hands. "I understand."

The guy trailed the tip of the gun against her hairline, as if caressing her, toying with her. Matt clenched his jaw so tight he thought it might snap.

Eli's sobs grew louder, more insistent.

"The baby?" Matt prompted.

Casting one last, sinister smile at Jenna, the man crossed the room. He pulled a small key out of his pocket and came up behind Matt, probably wanting to avoid a head butt or other aggressive move. Matt would never risk something like that until he was free of the cuffs.

The guy placed the metal key between Matt's fingers.

Then he stepped away, walking back to the sofa where he repositioned himself behind Jenna.

Matt unlocked the cuffs, stood and tossed them on the kitchen table. Rubbing his wrists, he went to Eli and kneeled. Inside his snowsuit he found the boy's pacifier hooked on a ribbon clipped to his overalls. "Here ya go, buddy." Matt popped it into Eli's mouth and unbuckled him.

"Leave him in the car seat," the guy ordered.

"Do you want him to stop crying or not?" Matt said.

The jerk raised an eyebrow and nodded at the gun aimed at Jenna.

"He won't stop crying unless I get him out of this wet diaper," Matt said.

The guy motioned toward the door where he'd dropped the diaper bag. Matt went to work by removing Eli's snowsuit and picking him up. "It's gonna be okay, buddy."

He grabbed the diaper bag on his way to the kitchen table, intensely aware of the gun pointed at Jenna's head.

The man made a phone call. "It's Veck. I need a pickup. My car's blocked. I'll text you the address… That's unacceptable." He glanced at Matt. "I've got them… No, I said ASAP… No guarantees." He hung up and texted something into his phone.

"What's this all about anyway?" Matt asked, unzipping the diaper bag and pulling out diapers and wipes. He'd continue to play the role of Matt the janitor and see how far that got him.

The bearded guy glanced briefly out the window.

"I never thought helping out a friend would be so dangerous," Matt said. "Any chance I'm gonna live through this?"

No answer. Matt lay Eli on the portable changing pad and removed the boy's pants to get to work on the fresh diaper.

"I mean, what do you want from an innocent woman like Jenna?" Matt said.

"Innocent? She kidnapped a kid."

Good, at least Matt had gotten him talking. That was his goal, get him talking and make him see Matt, Jenna and Eli as human beings, not as an assignment.

"Eli's mother asked Jenna to protect him."

"This woman's unstable," the man said. "I've been hired to retrieve her and the child."

"Who hired you?"

"You ask a lotta questions."

Matt secured the new diaper in place. "Can you blame me? You choke me unconscious, handcuff me to a beam and now you're threatening to kill Jenna. All I did was help out a friend."

"This friend got you in a pile of trouble."

"Yeah, well, I'm guessing if you were going to kill us you would have done so by now."

"Don't test me."

Matt picked up the little boy and rocked from side to side to comfort him.

"Buh-buh," Eli said, with a whimper.

Matt spotted the white bear in his diaper bag. "You want this?" He pulled it out and nuzzled it against the kid's cheek.

"He's quiet. Put him back in the car seat," the guy ordered.

"He'll just start wailing again." Matt rocked Eli and made his way across the cabin toward Jenna.

"Stay back." The guy aimed his gun at Matt and Eli.

Matt hesitated. "You seriously think I'm gonna pull a ninja move while holding this child? I want to check on Jenna."

"She's got a pulse."

Matt took a step closer and noticed redness forming below her eye and blood seeping from a cut above her hairline.

"You've seen her. Get back."

Matt did as ordered, considering his next move. With his thumb pressing against his fingertips, Eli tapped his mouth with a whimper. The little boy was hungry.

"Got you covered, big guy." Matt dug in the diaper bag and pulled out a multigrain bar, squeezable applesauce and crackers.

"Don't suppose you'd go get the cooler from the truck?" Matt asked the assailant.

The guy narrowed his eyes.

"Didn't think so." Matt put Eli down and opened the applesauce.

Thanks to the snacks, Eli wasn't fussing anymore. With wide eyes, he held the applesauce container and sucked it down.

"How much trouble did I get into by being a good friend?" Matt asked the guy.

The bearded man shook his head.

"That bad, huh?"

The guy shrugged.

"Can you at least tell me who's behind all this?"

"They need the kid. That's all I know."

But why? That's what Matt couldn't figure out.

"No, Joey, no," Jenna muttered, thrashing from side to side. "I can't… My baby," she groaned with an emotional intensity that ripped through Matt's chest.

"Joey…no!" She sat straight up, sobs racking her body.

"What's wrong with her?" the thug said.

Matt picked up Eli, who gripped the applesauce in one hand and his bear in the other. "Jenna, you had a nightmare," he said. "Open your eyes."

"My baby, he's gone… My baby," she cried, rocking back and forth, while squeezing her head between her hands.

"Jenna, look at me." Matt kneeled beside her. He wasn't sure what was going on, but he had to shake her out of this devastating spin. "Sweetheart, open your eyes. Eli needs you."

"My baby?" she whispered.

"No, Eli, remember?" Matt encouraged.

With a half gasp, she looked at Eli, and her brows knit together in a confused frown.

"It's okay. We're all okay," Matt said.

She studied Eli as if she knew something was wrong, that he wasn't the child she'd cried out for, but couldn't make sense of who Eli was.

"Buh-buh." Eli reached out with his hand and tapped Jenna's nose with his bear.

"That's right, Eli, Bubba will make it better," Matt said.

Jenna blinked and a tear trailed down her cheek.

"It's okay," Matt said.

She shook her head and flopped back down on the sofa.

"That's it. Relax." He stroked her blond hair with one hand, while holding Eli with the other. A few minutes later her breathing slowed and she'd fallen back asleep.

Eli swung the bear at Jenna, but Matt caught it before it made contact. Rest was what she needed. The longer she slept, the longer she'd be at peace and not realize the severity of their situation.

He released Eli, who toddled across the cabin toward the kitchen. Matt followed him, baby-proofing along the way. His thoughts were absorbed with Jenna's desperate cry for Joey.

"What was that about?" the thug asked.

"Haven't a clue."

"Uh-huh. You called her *sweetheart*."

He couldn't help it; the endearment had slipped out. "So what's next?" Matt pressed.

"They're coming to get us." He shot a quick glance out the window at the intensifying snowstorm.

The weather would delay his associates' arrival, whoever they were, hopefully giving Matt time to figure out how to get the advantage over the assailant without putting Jenna and Eli at risk.

Yeah, and how was he going to do that? He suspected Jenna suffered from a concussion and that's what had caused her to confuse Eli with a child named Joey. She was so vulnerable, to both her past and the cruelty of the man standing behind her. Matt clenched his jaw against the anger eating him up inside.

Crazed emotions weren't going to save them from this mercenary. Matt had to push his worry aside and come up with a plan.

Casting all your care upon Him; for He careth for you.

A few hours later darkness blanketed the remote Montana countryside. The snowstorm had developed into a full-on blizzard.

The assailant seemed edgy, pacing from window to window. Of course he was anxious. This assignment wasn't going anywhere near as planned. He'd been hired to retrieve Jenna and the little boy, but instead was stuck in a cabin with an incoherent woman, an energetic toddler and Matt, an unknown who could potentially overpower him.

It probably didn't help that at this moment Eli was being incredibly cute, toddling from one piece of furniture to the next, burning off energy from eating applesauce, crackers and two multigrain bars for dinner. Even a hardened man like this mercenary wasn't immune to Eli's charm.

The guy kept checking his phone, firing off text messages, probably demanding his associates plow through the storm to get to him ASAP.

Eli started fussing, flopping down on the floor and crying in between gasps of breath. It was obviously bedtime.

Matt changed Eli's diaper. "He's ready for bed."

The guy narrowed his eyes, as if trying to discern Matt's strategy.

"I'm going to put him down in the bedroom," Matt said.

"He can sleep here."

"With all these lights on?"

"Fine, put him to bed."

His tone actually sounded pleasant. Little Eli might have crept his way into the guy's heart.

"But don't do anything stupid." He pointed the gun at Jenna.

On the other hand…

"It might take me a few minutes." Matt gently picked up the fussy child. Eli whimpered and rubbed his eyes with a clenched fist.

Matt went into the bedroom and shut the door. His first instinct was to look for a way out, but he shoved that thought aside considering the reality of his situation.

Matt, Jenna and Eli were captives of a mercenary without a soul. Even if Matt fled the cabin, he'd never make it far in a blizzard, and he couldn't leave Jenna behind.

"Let's get you settled." He clicked off the overhead light and turned on a bedside lamp, submerging the room in semidarkness.

Not wanting to put Eli on the bed for fear he'd roll off, Matt shoved the mattress onto the floor. He pulled back the comforter and laid Eli down. The boy kicked his feet and cried out, not wanting to sleep, unwilling to miss the action.

Matt lay down beside Eli and rubbed the furry polar bear against the boy's nose. "What's Bubba doin'? Is he kissing you?"

The boy blinked teary eyes at Matt.

"Kiss, kiss, kiss," Matt whispered.

While trying to calm the little boy into sleep, another part of his mind drifted to Jenna.

She hadn't awakened since her nightmare about Joey a few hours ago. Matt hoped she didn't wake up while he was in here with Eli. He didn't know what Jenna would do if she thought something had happened to Eli, that someone had taken him.

Matt hummed to the little boy while his brain fired off questions. How had the bearded guy known Jenna and Matt were on their way? Had they been wrong to trust Marcus? Or were they being tracked somehow?

This wasn't the time to figure out who'd had a role in this. He needed to soothe Eli to sleep and develop a plan for a safe escape.

That gave him an idea. Since Marcus was a former SEAL turned security professional, he would no doubt keep weapons in the cabin. Matt could use a firearm right about now.

Eli rolled onto his tummy, stuck his bottom up in the air and sucked intently on his pacifier. Matt stroked his back, whispering, "Good boy, such a good boy."

A few minutes later, Eli stopped fussing and Matt removed his hand. The boy didn't stir. He had drifted into a deep sleep.

Matt eased off the mattress and quietly searched the room for a weapon. With Eli in here, Matt might have a chance to rescue Jenna and take down the assailant in the living room.

A slim chance if he wanted to avoid Jenna getting shot in the process.

Opening the dresser drawers, he sifted through Marcus's clothes, but found nothing.

He moved on to the closet because that's where Matt kept his lockbox for his gun. He glanced at Eli, still sound asleep. Matt searched the top shelf. Nothing. He kneeled and tapped on the closet floor searching for a secret compartment, but it was solid.

Where would Marcus keep his firearm?

Matt stood and scanned the room.

A trained soldier would want easy and quick access, and might not worry about locking it up because he didn't have children living with him.

Footsteps echoed from the next room.

Matt repositioned himself beside Eli.

The door cracked open, and light from the living area poured into the room.

"Shh," Matt said, stroking the boy's back.

The guy peeked at Eli. As if he thought Matt was going to abscond with the child out the window into a blizzard.

"Close the door," Matt said.

The man's eye twitched with frustration, but he closed the door.

Matt stood and continued to search for a gun. Checking the nightstand, he found a flashlight. That would come in handy.

He grabbed it and froze. Thought he heard something.

The roar of an engine outside.

Not good. The bearded guy's men were closing in.

Matt concentrated on finding a weapon. He dropped to the floor and searched beneath the bed, aiming the beam of light left, then right across the floor.

Nothing.

As the engine grew louder, Matt realized it sounded more like a snowmobile.

The engine stopped. They were just outside.

Matt lay flat on his back and pointed the flashlight beam up, beneath the bed.

"Bingo." In a holster attached to the underside of the metal frame was a firearm.

"Good man," he whispered, reaching for it. Just as he heard a scream.

"No! Let me go!" Jenna cried out.

EIGHT

Matt ripped the gun out of its holster and bolted across the bedroom. He hesitated. Charging in there with guns blazing wasn't going to help any of them. A squeak from Eli drew his attention to the sleeping child.

He had to be smart about this. Needed to know what he was dealing with before he took aggressive action.

Cracking the door open, he peered into the living room. Instead of multiple men storming the cabin, the bearded guy stood behind Jenna with a gun to her back. He was dragging her toward the front door.

"Tell them you're friends with the owner," the bearded guy ordered.

So these were not *his* men? Interesting.

"The owner?" Jenna seemed out of it, disoriented. She stumbled as she reached the door, bracing herself with an open palm against the sturdy wood.

"Don't mess up," the bearded guy growled.

"Where's Joey?" she asked.

"Who?"

"I mean Eli—where's Eli?" She snapped around to glare at the guy.

Pretty gutsy.

"Your friend's got him in the other room."

She started to look toward the bedroom, but the guy smacked the back of her head with an open palm.

"Hey!" she shouted.

Matt would certainly need to pray for self-control if he ever got this jerk alone.

"Everything okay in there?" a muffled voice called through the main door.

Matt gripped the gun. Watching, waiting. He was ready.

She opened the cabin door. "Yes?"

"Ma'am, I'm Officer Patterson with the county PD. Do you live here?"

"No, I'm… I'm visiting my friend, Marcus."

"Is everything okay? You look—" he paused "—upset."

"I… I was asleep."

"Oh, I'm sorry to have disturbed you."

"That's okay."

Matt hoped the cop would leave so he could take care of the bearded guy without putting the cop in danger.

"Ma'am, are you alone?"

"No, my friend Matt is here with me."

"May I meet him, please?"

Jenna glanced over her shoulder at the assailant.

Matt held his breath. Now what? If Matt came out of hiding, the bearded guy would shoot the cop and possibly Jenna.

The bearded guy eased his gun into the back of his jeans and opened the door wide. "Officer," he greeted the policeman.

"Matt…?"

"Tomlin."

Yet he'd identified himself as Veck when he'd called for backup.

"The storm's not letting up for at least forty-eight hours," the cop said. "I hope Marcus left a fully stocked pantry."

Something felt off about the conversation. Matt wondered if the cop was a rookie, unable to sense danger. He continued to stand there, making small talk.

Behind him, Matt heard the window slide open. He shut the bedroom door and spun around, aiming his weapon at a man on the other side of the window. The guy pressed his forefinger to his lips, indicating they should be quiet. Matt didn't lower his weapon.

The man, midthirties with dark hair and eyes, climbed through the window and gazed down at the sleeping boy.

"That must be Eli," he whispered, and then looked at Matt. "I see you found my favorite piece. Under the bed frame on the right side?"

Matt lowered the weapon. "Marcus?"

He nodded, peeled back a rug and popped open a hidden door. He pulled out a duffel bag and slung it over his shoulder. "Officer Patterson's a friend. He's supposed to figure out how many guys broke into my place."

"You knew they broke in?"

"Got an alert on my phone. What are we looking at?"

"One guy, not afraid to kill."

"Neither am I."

"My priority is to protect the woman and child."

"Me too. When Patterson leaves, go back into the living room and protect the woman. Eli will be safe in here. I'll take care of the rest."

Marcus motioned for the gun. "My piece?"

Matt shook his head, still not a hundred percent sure this guy was solid.

"You can't take that into the living room," Marcus said.

Matt studied him but didn't give up the gun.

"You don't trust me. Fair enough," Marcus said. "Just know I'm really good at what I do." He climbed out the window and disappeared into the dark night.

A few minutes later, the vibration from the

front door slamming indicated Officer Patterson had left. Matt placed the gun on top of a row of books just as the door to the bedroom opened.

Jenna stepped inside, but only partially. The thug was holding on to her arm. “Is Eli okay?” she asked.

“Yeah, he’s sleeping.” Matt went to her and squeezed her hand. “Everything’s fine.”

She still seemed out of it. The thug released her and motioned them to the sofa. Once there, Matt put his arm around her shoulder and pulled her close. She didn’t fight him. The sound of a snowmobile echoed through the window.

“She’s a smart girl,” the bearded guy said. “She followed orders.” He glanced out the window.

“I woke up and Eli wasn’t here.” Jenna looked into Matt’s eyes. “You weren’t here.”

“I’m sorry,” he said. “Eli needed to sleep. He’s one tired little tiger.”

“I should have been awake. I should have helped you.”

“Rest is the best thing for a concussion. A wise person once told me that.”

They shared an awkward smile, remembering when Jenna had given Matt that very advice after he’d been assaulted at the truck stop.

“What if he wakes up?” Jenna said, glancing over her shoulder at the bedroom door.

“He’s out. Trust me.”

She nodded and repositioned her head against

his shoulder. He pulled her tighter against him, readying himself for whatever Marcus was planning.

The anxiety that pinged through Jenna like a pinball seemed to wane the longer she leaned against Matt—a good thing because she needed to find clarity, and she needed to get grounded again. Her head injury had messed up her thinking, like it had years ago after Anthony took out his rage on her.

When she'd awakened earlier she'd been snagged by a memory: She was in the hospital crying out for a son she'd never know on this earth.

Anger bubbled up inside her. She would not let this vile bully hurt Eli. She started to sit up, but Matthew whispered, "Shh, it's going to be okay."

She studied his warm blue eyes, eyes that radiated hope and faith. How was he able to do that?

"How's your head?" he asked.

"It aches but I'm okay, I think."

The lights clicked off and they were suddenly plunged into darkness. Matt rolled them both onto the floor and shielded Jenna by wrapping his body around her.

"Get over here." The bearded guy scrambled across the cabin and tried to grab Jenna, but couldn't get past Matthew.

She heard Matthew grunt as the guy kicked him, but Matt wasn't letting go.

The cabin door slammed against the wall.

A gunshot rang out.

She yelped.

"It's okay," Matthew said against her ear.

Heart pounding with panic, she closed her eyes.

Tried to pray.

She couldn't remember any scripture, anything that could help calm her nerves.

"Casting all your care upon Him; for He careth for you," Matthew said, as if he sensed her need to reach out to God.

She repeated the phrase in her mind over and over during what felt like hours of a violent struggle.

Then, just as suddenly, silence blanketed the room.

"You guys okay?" a man asked.

The lights clicked on.

"Looks like you're just fine," the guy said with a touch of humor in his voice.

Matthew released Jenna and helped her sit up. They both leaned against the sofa.

A stranger stood beside the door, his boot resting on the bearded guy's back. The thug's wrists were bound and he grunted in protest.

"Jenna," Matthew said. "This is Marcus."

"Marcus, wow." She glanced around the room,

noting the overturned chairs and broken lamp. "How did you…?"

He pointed to goggles on the top of his head. "Night vision." He glanced at the thug. "Didn't stand a chance."

Jenna cocked her head. She thought she heard…

Yep. Eli was crying.

"Go ahead," Matt said.

That's when she realized he was holding her hand. It felt natural and comforting.

It felt good.

"Thanks," she said, but didn't want to let go.

He released her hand. "Hope I didn't crush you."

"You didn't." In truth, she'd felt safer than she had in a long time. Thanks to a man's protection. She never thought she'd feel that way. Ever.

"Want me to check on him?" Matthew offered, probably wondering about her hesitation.

"No, I'm good." She glanced at Marcus. "Thanks for the save."

"Sure. So what's going on with my cousin Chloe?"

Jenna's safe feeling was ripped out from under her. "She…"

"I'll explain everything," Matthew said. "Go to Eli."

"Thanks." She didn't want to relive the memory, the fear.

Fear. She needed to seriously deal with that emotion so it wouldn't consume her every thought, especially if she was about to comfort a child.

She opened the bedroom door and went to Eli. She touched his lips with the Binky, which had fallen out of his mouth. He latched on to it, but still whimpered.

She wasn't sure what the official pacifier rules were regarding at what age a child should relinquish it, but she figured he deserved every comfort she could offer considering the circumstances.

"Bubba, my bubba," she said, making up a song. "I love my baby bubba." She stroked his cheek with the stuffed animal. He rolled onto his side and grabbed the bear. Jenna continued to sing, and Eli kept sucking on his pacifier. His eyelids drifted closed.

The gunshot must have awakened him. Poor child. She hoped he didn't have nightmares from everything that was happening.

For half a second she wondered if she was doing the right thing, or if she should take Eli back to his father.

Gary is a monster, Chloe had said.

Jenna had experienced her share of those, yet couldn't remember ever experiencing kindness from a peaceful, compassionate man.

Until now.

Until Matthew.

As she sang to Eli, she wondered what would happen next. The bearded guy's associates were still on their way, which made Jenna, Matthew and Eli easy targets. They should flee the cabin and take refuge elsewhere. How long could they keep running, and how would they escape with a snowstorm barreling down on the countryside?

Panic threatened to take hold. Then she remembered Matthew's words: *Casting all your care upon Him...*

Yes, that's what she'd do. She'd surrender her worry to God.

As she stroked the little boy's hairline, she continued to whisper sweet words.

"Precious little boy, you are so very loved."

For the briefest of moments, she thought she felt a flicker of love from God touch her heart.

...for He careth for you.

She considered the last few hours, how she'd survived a car accident and being held hostage. How Marcus showed up in time to help them, and the incredible peace she'd found in Matthew's arms.

Was God looking out for her? Had her subconscious prayers, in fact, been answered?

With a sigh and a squeak, Eli rolled onto his tummy, his butt up in the air, clutching the white bear against his cheek. She covered him with the blanket and stroked the back of his head, humming softly.

Thank you, God, for protecting this beautiful child.

As the minutes passed, she was distracted by the sound of low male voices drifting from the other room. She took a deep breath, finding strength to deal with Marcus's grief when she rejoined them. Could God help with that as well? Could He help her be there for Marcus without the man's grief pulling Jenna down into the darkness?

That's when it hit her that all these years since she'd left Anthony, she'd been running from darkness and grief, from any and all conflict. Yet, along with joy, these were a part of the human experience. She admitted she hadn't truly dealt with the darkness haunting her—she hadn't dealt fully with her violent past, which meant she hadn't healed and couldn't move on.

The past would haunt her indefinitely. As long as she allowed it to.

In essence, she was letting Anthony control not only her present, but also her future.

That thought made her angry, but in a good way. It wasn't a victim-like anger, it was a warrior-type outrage, the kind that builds strength from within, inspires a person to stand up for herself and not back down from a fight.

To not back down from fear.

Convinced Eli had drifted off into a sound sleep, Jenna slid off the mattress. She made a makeshift wall around the edge of the bed with pillows and blankets. Standing up, she hovered beside the little boy and felt a surge of strength pour through her.

Strength, determination and courage.

She quietly crossed the room, hesitated at the door and took a deep breath. "Please, God, help me be strong."

For Eli, for Marcus and for herself.

She stepped into the living room and gently shut the door behind her. Matthew was sitting at the kitchen table. The bearded thug and Marcus were gone.

"Officer Patterson took him into custody," Matthew said, in answer to her unspoken question.

"And Marcus?"

"Helping escort the guy to Patterson's patrol car. It's parked on the main road."

"Do we need to leave?"

"Not right away. Marcus and I checked the assailant's text messages. His men were delayed by weather. We sent a response text from our bearded friend claiming that he was able to get his car out after all and he's on his way. That'll buy us some time."

"His car?"

"Apparently you blocked it when you banked the truck."

"Oh, right. I'm not sure how much damage I did to Ed's truck. Sorry."

"Come sit down." Matthew motioned to her. "Coffee's brewing, or tea if you'd prefer."

"I'll get some in a minute." She crossed the room and placed her hand on Matthew's shoulder. "Thank you, again, for everything."

She wondered if he sensed that her gratitude went far deeper than saving her and Eli's lives, that he'd been able to do something she didn't think possible—offer her peace.

"That sounds ominous," Matthew said.

She searched his blue eyes. "What do you mean?"

"It sounds like you're saying goodbye."

"No, that's not what I meant."

But they both knew the goal had been to find Marcus, who would take over protecting Jenna and Eli.

"How's Eli?" Matthew changed the subject.

"Good, asleep." She shifted onto a chair next to him. "He's such a trooper."

"That he is. And you?"

She absently touched her forehead where she felt a bruise forming. "I have a little bit of a headache, but my vision's okay."

"That's not what I meant. Who's Joey?"

"Joey." She hesitated. "Joey was my unborn

son. He died after Anthony shoved me down the stairs."

Matthew touched her hand. "I am so sorry, Jenna."

She nodded.

"Anthony went to jail for homicide?" he asked.

"No, aggravated domestic battery."

"But you lost your child."

"I needed to extricate myself from his abuse as quickly as possible and wanted to avoid a public trial. He wouldn't plead guilty to homicide, but agreed to plead guilty to domestic battery. He spends three years in jail in exchange for a quick divorce. I wish the pain had been quick as well, but it will always linger."

He squeezed her hand in a compassionate gesture. But she didn't want this to turn into a pity party. "Did you tell Marcus about Chloe?"

"Yes. He blames himself for not taking her more seriously."

"What do you mean?"

"She sent him an email last week stating she wanted to flee with Eli."

"And he ignored her?" she said, unable to keep the judgment from her voice.

"According to Marcus, Chloe tended to be dramatic at times." He glanced at Jenna. "Did you find that to be true?"

"I suppose a little, but that doesn't negate her feelings."

"Agreed. Yet if someone constantly sounds the alarm, after a while people start to hear nothing but white noise." He pursed his lips.

"Why do I sense you're speaking from personal experience?"

Matthew shrugged. "I think the coffee's ready. Or did you want tea?"

"Tea would be great."

He went to the hot water kettle and she watched him scoop instant coffee into two mugs, put a teabag in a third and pour hot water into all three. He rejoined her at the table and slid the tea in front of her.

"Thanks." She wrapped her fingers around the mug. "So, we were talking about overly dramatic people who cry wolf. Does that have anything to do with—" she hesitated "—Sarah?"

He snapped his gaze to meet hers, but she didn't see anger there or even irritation. Sadness dulled his blue eyes instead.

"I'm sorry. It's none of my business." She dipped her teabag in and out of the mug a few times.

"How did you know about Sarah?"

"When you were injured at the truck stop, you said her name. You apologized to her."

He stared into his coffee. "She was my almost fiancée."

"Almost?"

"The night I'd planned to propose, she got in a car accident and died."

"Oh, Matthew." She reached over and touched his hand wrapped around the coffee mug.

"At the time, I blamed myself," he said.

"What? Why?"

"The night I proposed, we got in a fight and she tore off in a crazy state. She wasn't paying attention to the road, was driving too fast for the conditions and got hit by a truck."

"Why would you blame yourself?"

"I should have been more considerate of her feelings, I guess. Instead, I thought she was being selfish and overreacting."

"To what?"

"My job, how dangerous and demanding it is. When I worked an undercover assignment, I could go months without seeing her and she'd worry herself into a state. She knew when we started dating what she was signing on for, and I think she liked it, being able to say she was dating an FBI agent. I never pretended to be a nine-to-five kind of guy." He glanced up at Jenna. "Sorry. I don't know why I'm telling you all this."

"I'm glad you are." She squeezed his hand, encouraging him to continue.

"Anyway, I thought a marriage proposal might help ease her fears, but instead she lost it. Started shouting about two people making a marriage, not one, that she'd be raising our children on her own, that she'd have to give up her career as a physical therapist. I thought I was doing the right thing by proposing..." His voice trailed off.

"Of course you were. You loved her."

He glanced at Jenna with regret in his eyes. "I should have gone after her that night."

"You couldn't have prevented the accident."

"No, but I could have stopped her from leaving in such a crazed state."

"We all have regrets about what might have happened if we'd made a different choice."

He nodded and sipped his coffee.

"May I ask, why didn't you stop her? I don't mean that to sound judgmental."

He shook his head. "I spent a year and a half asking myself that same question, praying on it, praying for forgiveness."

"Did you get it?"

"Yes, but I had to face an ugly truth. I was actually relieved she wanted to break up. And then... well, I had to admit that we weren't meant to be together, but I couldn't bring myself to break up because she needed me, she needed someone with integrity, someone to take care of her. She'd been emotionally damaged by her father and other men in her life. I didn't know that until we were together for a couple of months. She was good at hiding her emotional scars with humor."

Jenna wondered if that's why Matthew had assigned himself as her protector, because he had a driving need to protect women.

"Do you still blame yourself for her accident?" Jenna asked.

"Actually, no." He sat back in his chair. "I've learned you can't control other people's choices, but you should pay close attention to what's going on, you know, be present."

"That's what I was doing with Chloe when she came to see me."

"You're a good friend," Matthew offered.

"Maybe."

Matthew cocked his head in question.

"A better friend would have been able to save her life," she said.

"In those circumstances you would have been overpowered. There's nothing you could have done."

Jenna shrugged. A few seconds of silence stretched between them. It wasn't uncomfortable silence, but contemplative.

"What happens next?" she asked. "Will you be heading back to the community center?"

"You're that anxious to get rid of me, huh?" He winked.

On the contrary, she dreaded the moment he left her and Eli, even though she was confident in Marcus's ability to protect them.

"I assumed once we found Marcus that you'd

go back to your normal, undercover life," she said. "That sounded weird, didn't it?"

That charming half smile tugged at his lips. "Let's confer with Marcus before we make our next move. He knows the area and the local law enforcement, and he's obviously pretty good with strategy."

Marcus reentered the cabin, tapping his boots on the rug by the door. "The guy's name is Brian Veck. Mean anything to either of you?"

"No," Matthew said.

Jenna shook her head.

"Patterson will run him through the database to see if anything pops." Marcus shucked his jacket and hung it on the coatrack. "He's charging Veck with breaking and entering, kidnapping, assault and attempted murder."

"Attempted murder?" Jenna echoed.

"Yeah, he tried to kill me—oh, wait, you didn't see it because the lights were out." Marcus smiled.

"Your coffee's on the counter," Matthew said.

"Thanks." Marcus grabbed the mug and leaned against the kitchen counter. "I still can't believe what happened to Chloe."

"I'm so sorry, Marcus," Jenna said.

"What did she get herself into?"

"I think it's related to a money-laundering case I'm working on," Matthew offered.

"She left me a voice mail about wanting to

leave Gary, but I was running a protective detail for a family overseas and had to stay focused. I emailed her that I'd get in touch when I returned to the States." He shook his head. "I can protect complete strangers, but can't even take care of my own family."

"No one could have known her life was in danger," Jenna said. "I certainly didn't."

"Why Chloe?" Marcus glanced at Jenna, and she had to steel herself against his painful expression.

"I think her husband was involved in the money laundering somehow," Matthew said.

"Okay, but why kill *her*?" Marcus pressed.

"She probably knew too much. Either she heard something or saw something she shouldn't have," Matthew said.

"She was certainly scared when she came to see me," Jenna said.

"And now it sounds like your life is in danger." Marcus nodded at Jenna. "But what do they want with Eli?"

"Gary obviously wants his son back," Jenna said.

"Not happening, not if he's in any way responsible for my cousin's death." Marcus turned to Matthew. "You're going after Gary, right?"

"That's why I was undercover at the foundation's office, to determine who was involved and find evidence to support our case."

"Then you need to get back there and put the guy away. I'll protect Jenna and Eli."

Matthew glanced at Jenna and she nodded her approval of the plan, even though her heart panged with the anticipated loss of a good friend.

A friend? Really, Jenna?

"Is that what you want?" Matthew asked her.

No, of course not.

"Yes," she said. "If it will put an end to the threat against Eli."

Matthew ripped his gaze from Jenna and addressed Marcus. "I figure we've got until tomorrow morning before they come looking for Veck."

"I'll keep watch tonight. I'm jet-lagged anyway, so night is my daytime. You two get some sleep."

"I'll get the portable playpen from the truck for Eli, and Jenna can take the bed." Matthew crossed the room and put on his coat.

It was almost like he needed to get away from Jenna, to put distance between them. He hesitated before opening the door, as if he wanted to say something to her. Instead, he left and shut the door behind him.

The next morning Jenna did her best to be strong as she played with Eli, even though her heart was breaking.

Matthew had left without saying a final goodbye. Once he'd clicked into agent mode, he apparently couldn't be distracted by feelings that had grown between him and Jenna.

Or maybe she was kidding herself and the feelings were one-sided.

No, they'd obviously grown close or else he wouldn't have opened up so completely about Sarah's death. He'd claimed that he had forgiven himself for the accident, but Jenna wasn't so sure.

For one thing, she was puzzled by the idea of self-forgiveness.

Marcus entered the cabin. "Looks like a good day ahead. Sun's shining. Main road's clear. I'm able to track Veck's main contact through his phone. They're a solid six hours away." He went to the kitchen. "I've got surveillance set up around the property so we'll know if anyone's coming."

"That's great," she said, continuing to play blocks with Eli.

"Once we got the truck out of the snowbank, and changed the tire, it started up just fine. There was a little damage to the fender, but nothing serious. That was a good move, to block the drive so the thug couldn't get out."

"It wasn't intentional."

"Matt was sorry he missed you this morning. He hopes to get back to Cedar River by midday."

"Good, that's good." Except *good* didn't describe how she felt at this very moment.

"It's normal, ya know."

She glanced at him. "What's that?"

"To develop a connection to someone who's protecting you."

"How did you…?"

"It's my business, remember? Protecting people."

"So I'll stop missing him after a while?"

"Sure, no doubt."

His response didn't sound convincing.

"How's my little cousin doing?" Marcus grabbed Eli and held him up like he was flying. Eli giggled and kicked his feet. Marcus put the boy down and tugged on his overalls. "Very stylish, dude."

Eli giggled, turned and ran back to the coffee table to play with his blocks.

"What's the plan?" she asked.

"My buddy has a place near the Idaho border. I'll take you there and we'll wait it out until we hear back from Matt."

"I hope we're not interfering with your work schedule."

"No problem. I got it covered."

He grabbed his phone and eyed the screen. "That's not good."

Jenna sat up.

He grabbed a pair of binoculars off a bookshelf and looked through the front window. "Whoa, you've gotta go."

"Me, what about you?"

He calmly picked up Eli's snowsuit and Jenna's jacket. "Get the diaper bag."

"Who's here?"

He pinned her with steely dark eyes. "If you want to survive, you'll need to follow my orders."

She nodded and went into the bedroom to get the baby's diaper bag. Although tempted to look out the window to see what was happening, she knew time was critical and that her best option was to follow Marcus's orders.

When she reentered the living room, she noticed wooden boards were pulled up, exposing a hole in the floor by the fireplace.

"That's my safe room," he said, by way of explanation. "It opens to a tunnel that leads to the shed out back. Take Eli to the shed and wait until someone comes to get you. I'd suggest you use the snowmobile back there, but that'd be impossible to manage with a kid."

"Wait, a safe room? With a tunnel?"

"The shed's not heated, but you'll be okay in your snow gear. I'll text Patterson to retrieve you, okay?"

"But who's out there?"

"Looks like the Feds, but I can't know for sure. Go on," he said calmly.

"But Marcus—"

"Chloe chose you to protect Eli because you're strong, Jenna. You can do this."

With a nod, she climbed down the stairs to the

safe room and he handed her Eli. Then he tossed their snow gear down and pointed. "Switch is on the left."

She felt around and flicked it on. A soft glow illuminated a room full of supplies, including weapons, food and water.

"Follow the tunnel to the shed," Marcus repeated.

She glanced nervously toward the dark opening leading into the tunnel.

"Flashlight is by the entrance, see it?"

She nodded, but couldn't speak past the fear tightening her throat.

"Oh, and Jenna—"

Pounding echoed from the front door.

"Go, go." He shut the trap door.

She stared at it for a few seconds, gathering her thoughts…and her courage.

Please, God, give me courage.

With a sudden rush of purpose, she got Eli dressed in his snow jacket. She put on her own jacket and scarf, keeping a close eye on him as she fumbled around the small room.

"Let's go, buddy," she said.

She strapped Eli in the baby carrier, positioning him against her chest. "Ready for an adventure?" she said brightly, because she knew children sensed your emotions, your fear, and would react accordingly.

"Buh-buh," he said. She grabbed the white bear

out of the diaper bag and handed it to him. The little boy snatched it and giggled, burying his face into the soft fur.

She aimed the flashlight into the tunnel. “I can do this.”

The ground was covered with wooden planks that served as a floor, and the walls were braced with beams. A quick flash of it collapsing made Jenna hesitate for a moment.

With a determined breath, she stepped into the dark passageway, hearing Marcus’s words echo in her mind—*Chloe chose you to protect Eli because you’re strong, Jenna.*

“I am strong.”

As she forged ahead, she heard pounding from above, then the sound of men shouting, someone giving loud orders, and more pounding. She blockcd out the distraction, determined to reach her goal: getting to safety and waiting for Marcus’s friend, Officer Patterson, to come get her.

In the meantime, she’d keep Eli happy and distracted in the shed. She pushed aside the thought that the men would come looking for her there.

“Isn’t this something, Eli?”

His eyes widened and he looked around. Fueled by determination, and love for this innocent child, Jenna focused on the ladder in the distance.

She picked up her pace, ignoring the walls that felt like they were closing in, the darkness barreling down on her from behind.

Approaching the end of the tunnel, she set the flashlight on the ground, pointing it upward. The beam illuminated a door up above.

"Here we go, buddy." She ascended the ladder, hoping the door would easily open. She didn't want to think about being stuck down here.

She tapped on the door. "Help Jenna, buddy."

Eli reached out and tapped as well.

"One, two, three..."

She pushed it open with ease, and relief poured through her. She climbed up into the shed and took Eli out of the carrier. Shucking the diaper and her messenger bags, she scanned the shed for anything immediately dangerous to Eli. Because the supplies were locked in tall metal cabinets, it seemed pretty safe.

There was one window, facing the cabin, which had probably been designed for Marcus to keep an eye on what was happening if he ever needed to escape and hide out in here. A few minutes later, she noticed two dark SUVs driving away from the property toward the main road.

Driving away? Which meant...they'd taken Marcus?

Eli hugged her leg and let out a squeal. He was bored, or tired, or a little of both. It was about time for his midday nap. She put him back in the carrier, facing her.

"It's okay, baby boy. Everything's okay."

If only Matthew were here.

No, she had to learn to take care of herself and Eli without Matthew's help.

She rocked Eli from one side of the eight-by-eight shed to the other. He squealed and kicked his feet. She kept moving, humming, and he finally quieted down. She looked at his sweet face and realized he'd fallen asleep from the movement.

"We'll be okay," she whispered, stroking the back of his head.

She thought she heard a soft tap at the door. Officer Patterson had certainly arrived quickly.

She opened the door…

To the angry expression of Chloe's husband, Gary.

"What are you—?"

"I'll take my child now," he demanded.

NINE

No matter how hard Matt tried to convince himself that leaving Jenna behind was the right thing to do, he still felt like he'd made a colossal mistake.

Intellectually it made sense for him to return to his undercover assignment, to continue to expose the money laundering. That would essentially make Jenna safe again.

From Marcus's performance last night, Matt could tell the guy was equipped to handle any situation. Having confirmed Marcus's background with Bob Barnes yesterday made it easier for Matt to leave Jenna behind.

Not easy, but manageable. It was the best choice, especially given the circumstances and Bob's comment about Pragge threatening to dismiss agents who couldn't follow orders.

Matt's phone rang and he recognized Bob's number. He hit the speaker button. "Tell Pragge I'll be back at the foundation office tonight."

"Matt, it's about Marcus Garcia."

Matt gripped the wheel. "What about him?"

"There's a warrant out for his arrest."

"For what?"

"Assault and battery."

"I thought you said his background was clean."

"It was."

Matt slowed down and yanked the wheel left, doing a U-turn in the middle of the highway. "Why didn't you tell me this yesterday?"

"The warrant was issued this morning."

"When did this assault supposedly happen?" Matt asked.

"Last night."

"Impossible. He was with us."

Matt sped up, trying to control his panic, his frustration that he'd left Jenna when she needed him most.

"Who issued the warrant?" Matt asked.

"Cedar River PD."

"Chief Billings?"

"You got it."

Which meant they'd found a connection between Chloe and her cousin Marcus, and were closing in…

On Marcus and the cabin.

On Jenna and Eli.

"Is Jenna North okay?" Bob said.

"She will be."

"You're going back, aren't you?"

"Yep."

"What do you want me to tell Pragge?"

"Tell him I'll check in later."

Matt ended the call and hightailed it back to the cabin. He hadn't been driving all that fast when he'd left, a part of him not in any rush to return to his assignment.

Admit it, Matt, you didn't want to abandon Jenna.

He'd left the cabin half an hour ago, so if he doubled his speed he'd make it back in fifteen minutes.

"Hang in there, Jenna," he said, thankful that the plows had done good work overnight to clear the highway of snow.

With a bulletin out on Marcus, the authorities, local and national, would be on the lookout for him. That included Marcus's friend, Officer Patterson.

No one could be trusted.

Chief Billings no doubt figured with Marcus out of the way, Jenna would have no one to turn to.

How did they even find Marcus? It seemed like he stayed off the grid pretty well, and Matt was sure a guy like that would disable the GPS on his phone so as not to be tracked.

Then again, if they went through Chloe's phone and checked her email, they'd see she'd reached out to her cousin. Maybe they couldn't find him, but they knew he lived in Montana, and what better way to enlist the help of statewide police than to release a false bulletin?

Even if Officer Patterson remained loyal to Marcus, there were surely other officers who knew about the former Navy SEAL living in the area. People tended to know each other quite well in remote areas like this, sometimes their lives depending on being able to rely on neighbors.

He turned onto the long drive leading to the cabin. He didn't see any squad cars out front. Relaxing his fingers on the steering wheel, he took a deep breath. He'd make it back in time. They hadn't been discovered. Yet he still had to get to Marcus and let him know about the danger, danger that had put Jenna and Eli in the crosshairs as well.

He parked and rushed to the cabin. Knocked. No one answered. "Marcus!"

With a closed fist, he pounded on the door.

He darted left and looked through the window.

Marcus's chair that he'd used to keep watch was tipped over, a table lamp was on the floor and the rug was bunched in a corner.

"No," Matt ground out.

He went around and checked all the windows, trying to find a way in. The bedroom window was unlocked and he climbed inside.

The first thing he saw was the portable crib. They wouldn't have intentionally left this crucial piece of equipment behind. Which meant Jenna and Eli had been taken?

Or perhaps they'd fled the scene in a hurry, and the overturned furniture was the result of frustrated thugs who'd lost them again.

"Jenna, where are you?"

He went through the cabin looking for indications that they'd safely escaped. Then he heard it. Shouting.

It was coming from outside.

Matt pulled out his gun, left the cabin and made his way around back.

"We're not going with you!" Jenna cried out.

He spotted her being pulled through the snow by Gary McFadden. Eli, strapped into his carrier against her body, half squealed and half cried.

"We've got to get out of here!" Gary shouted.

"Think about your son!" she cried.

He spun around and got in her face. "That's right, he's my son! Mine!" He pointed at his own chest to make his point.

That's when Matt realized Gary gripped a gun in his hand.

"Let's go!" Gary yanked on her arm.

Where was he taking her? Didn't matter. Matt had to do something, and quick. He put away his gun, not wanting to escalate the situation, and trudged through the snow.

"Gary McFadden!" he called out, putting his hands up in a gesture of surrender.

The guy spun around and pointed the gun at Matt. Jenna looked surprised, and very relieved, to see Matt.

"Let Jenna go," Matt said.

"What are you doing here?"

"I'm FBI."

"You're a janitor," Gary scoffed.

"I'm undercover, and Jenna is under my protection, as is your son."

"I can protect my own son!" he shouted, as if trying to convince himself.

Eli burst into high-pitched wails. Still clutching the gun, Gary glanced at him. He released Jenna's arm and reached out to his son.

Jenna turned slightly in a protective stance.

"I'm supposed to protect him," Gary said in an oddly soft voice. "And Chloe."

Matt and Jenna shared a look. The man had gone from enraged to remorseful in less than two seconds.

"Gary, what's going on?" Jenna asked.

"I'm a dead man walking."

"What do you mean?" Jenna asked.

"You're right, Jenna. I'm a danger to my child." Gary touched the back of his son's head. "Please, don't let them hurt my boy."

"I get that you're scared," Matt said. "Let us help you."

Shaking his head, Gary said, "It's too late. I should have never gotten involved."

"It's the Guerro drug cartel, isn't it?"

Gary snapped his attention to Matt.

"Work with us. Help us shut them down," Matt said.

"No, I have to finish this. Make things right." He pressed a kiss on top of Eli's head. "You'll be okay, buddy. As long as you have your Bubba, you'll be okay."

"You can't keep running." Matt took a few steps closer.

"Stop." Gary pulled out the gun.

Jenna squinted and protected the child with her arms.

"I'd never hurt my boy." Gary glanced from Jenna to Matt and back to Jenna.

He must have realized his actions belied his proclamation because he lowered the weapon.

"Why are they after Eli?" Matt asked.

"Leverage. I want out. There is no getting out. And now I've put Eli's life in danger." With a defeated expression, Gary took a step back, then another.

That's when Matt noticed a snowmobile fifty yards away.

"You're right, Jenna. It's dangerous to be anywhere near me. I'm so sorry, Eli." Gary turned and trudged toward the snowmobile.

"Gary!" Matt shouted, and started after him.

"Forget about me! Love my son!" He climbed

onto the snowmobile, started it up and sped away before Matt could get to him.

Matt went to Jenna and hugged her, with the little boy between them.

"I can't believe you came back," she said against his shoulder. "What happened?"

"I found out there was a warrant on Marcus."

"I thought he was one of the good guys."

He broke the hug. "He is. The warrant was issued by Billings, who claims Marcus assaulted someone last night."

"But he was with us last night."

"Exactly. Let's go before we get more company." He started to lead her to the cabin.

"Wait, our stuff is in the shed."

They went back to the shed and grabbed the diaper and messenger bags. As they headed for the cabin, he was careful to help Jenna manage the snow. Although Marcus had shoveled a path early this morning, snow drifts covered part of the walkway now.

"What were you doing back here?" he asked.

"When the men in the SUVs came to get us, Marcus had me take a tunnel leading to the shed. He said he'd notify Officer Patterson to come to my aid."

"Considering the warrant, I'm not sure we can trust even him at this point. A tunnel, huh?"

"Yep, and a good thing, or I'd be wherever Marcus is right now."

"But you're not, you're okay."

"Are we?" she said. "They keep coming and we keep running. I'm not sure we'll ever be truly okay."

He wondered if she was talking about this particular situation, or if she was referring to her past.

"We've got more to work with now," Matt said. "Confirmation that Gary was involved with the money laundering will get my people on board with my plan."

"Which is?"

He glanced down into her brilliant green eyes. "To keep you and Eli safe."

"You're not going back to Cedar River?"

"No, ma'am."

"How can you work your case if you're not there?"

"Let me worry about that. For now, let's get someplace safe."

"I've heard that before." She snapped her attention to him. "Sorry, that wasn't meant as a criticism of your abilities."

"Maybe it should be."

"Matthew—"

"Hey, I think we know each other well enough that you can call me Matt."

"Matt, don't blame yourself for what just happened."

"I shouldn't have left you." They approached the cabin and he hesitated. "It won't happen again."

* * *

They packed the portable crib and supplies in Ed's truck and headed north toward the Canadian border. Jenna wasn't sure where they'd end up, and she didn't care much because at this moment she felt safe.

Thanks to Matthew.

Rather than judge herself for her growing dependence on him, she relaxed into the feeling. She'd learned from Patrice that stress and fear take a horrible toll on one's body, and that to fully heal, Jenna needed to embrace peace whenever possible.

Right now, with Matthew behind the wheel of the truck, and Eli asleep in the back seat, she felt a peaceful calm warm her body.

She sighed and found herself thanking God.

Matthew's faith must be wearing off on her.

"I'm going to stop at an ATM," he said.

"Won't they track your location?"

"They will, but from there we'll double back and go southwest, toward Idaho."

"What's in Idaho?"

"A cluster of cabins I heard about from a buddy of mine. We'll stay there until I can get backup."

"You mean, you're going to enlist the help of your counterparts at the FBI?"

"Yes."

Her peaceful moment was suddenly shattered. "Do you think that's a good idea?"

"We can't do this alone, Jenna. It's okay to ask for help. I thought you'd appreciate that more than anyone."

He was referring to her support from Gloria's Guardians. "Maybe I have a better idea."

"I'm listening."

"I'll call Patrice and see if we can stay with her for a while."

"That would be putting her in danger."

"She's a tough lady, and no one knows about the group, or my connection to it. We'd be safe there."

"At this point I'd rather not involve civilians."

"I understand, but these women are used to dealing with dangerous situations."

"Are you willing to risk exposing their service?"

She considered his comment.

"Let's go with my plan for now, okay?" he said.

She nodded. "What about Marcus?"

"I'll call my buddy at work and see if he can track down what happened to him."

"I hope he's okay."

"He's resourceful. I'm sure he's fine."

When they stopped at the ATM, she watched Matthew shield his face from the camera with the brim of his baseball cap.

He got back in the truck and they headed southwest. His phone rang on the dash cradle, a blocked number.

"Could be work," he said. He pressed the speaker button. "Weller."

"Matt? It's Chief Billings."

Jenna held her breath.

"Yes, Chief?" Matt said in a calm voice.

"Hope you don't mind me calling. I got your number from Kyle Armstrong."

"No problem. What can I do for you?"

Jenna glanced into the back seat at Eli, who had fallen asleep.

"I've got a few more questions about the break-in at the community center and was hoping to catch up with you today."

"Today's not good for me. How about tomorrow?"

A pregnant pause was followed by, "How about nine a.m.?"

"Sounds good."

"Officer Armstrong speaks very highly of you."

Matt glanced at the phone with a worried frown. "Thank you, sir."

"He's working on the break-in, tracking leads and looking for the man who assaulted you. Let's hope Officer Armstrong is as able to defend himself as you were."

"I'm sure he is, sir," Matthew said in a low voice. "Goodbye."

He hit the off button and smacked the palm of his hand against the steering wheel. "Unbelievable."

"What?" Jenna questioned.

"That was Billings's not-so-subtle threat that Kyle's life is in danger because of our friendship."

"Wait, no, he wouldn't hurt one of his own men," she said. "Would he?"

Matt shot her a look.

"What are you going to do?" she asked.

"I've gotta warn Kyle." He reached for the phone and hesitated. "How do I even explain this? I mean, I've been lying to him this whole time."

"It's your job as an undercover agent."

With a nod, he made the call.

"Hey, Matt," Kyle answered. "Missed you at coffee this morning."

"Yeah, sorry."

"You okay?"

"I need to talk to you about something important."

"Hang on. Yeah, Chief?"

Matt gripped the steering wheel.

"Sure thing. Okay, Matt, I'm back."

"I need you to listen to me very carefully."

"O-kay," he said with a half chuckle.

"You trust me, right?"

"Sure."

"Is Billings standing close by?"

"Yeah, why?"

Matt glanced at Jenna and shook his head. Jenna guessed he wouldn't share the information if there was a chance Billings could read Kyle's reaction.

"I'd better let you get back to work," Matt said, defeated.

"Not so fast. What's up?"

Matthew seemed to consider his options for a few seconds, and then he said, "I need you to do me a favor."

"Okay, as long as it's not hauling cement blocks to Hunter's farm again. My shoulders still ache from that favor," he joked.

"Kyle, I need you to read Jeremiah chapter twelve verse six. New Living Translation. Can you do that for me?"

"Odd request, but okay."

"Just between you and me. Don't even mention it to your chief."

"No problem. I doubt he'd be interested," he said.

"Thanks. And...be safe." Matt ended the call.

"Jeremiah chapter twelve verse six?" Jenna questioned.

"It's about your family, your brothers, turning against you."

By nightfall they'd reached their destination, the Lazy Shade Resort. Actually, it wasn't much of a resort, but more like a cluster of rustic cabins.

Matt booked a two-room cabin, complete with kitchenette, and paid for two nights with cash. He wasn't sure it was prudent to stay much longer than a couple of days.

It was a remote location and should be safe enough to give him time over the next forty-eight hours to work the case, to draw more connections between the cartel, Gary and Chief Billings.

The man who had threatened Matt's friend.

Matt rolled his neck, struggling to push his anger and worry aside. He had to have confidence that his friend would read and understand the message in the scripture.

He picked up supplies from the general store on the resort grounds, and went back to the cabin. He knocked four times and the door cracked open to Jenna's lovely face, her wide green eyes looking up at him.

She swung the door open and he spotted Eli leaning against the coffee table, playing with his stuffed bear and a plastic car.

"He seems pretty happy." Matt entered the cabin.

"I just gave him a bottle. I probably shouldn't be giving him bottles at this point, but it calms him down."

Matt cast one last glance outside and shut the door behind him.

"Hungry?" he asked, heading toward the kitchenette.

"Always hungry," she said.

The rental unit had an open living space with a separate bedroom, similar to Marcus's cabin.

"I bought canned beef stew, canned yams and pretzels."

"Hang on, I thought you were a health food guy."

"The store had a limited selection. Fresh fruit isn't delivered until the morning. Trust me, you didn't want me to bring home the wilted greens or overripe bananas."

She smiled, and he was lost for a second, lost in the fantasy of having a life with this woman.

For real. Not pretend, like this was.

Snap out of it, Weller.

"What else have you got there?" She peeked into the bag.

"Canned chicken à la king, in case you don't like beef."

"What's this?" She pulled a box of pancake mix out of the grocery bag.

"Breakfast."

"Why not dinner?" she said.

"Why not dinner," he repeated.

Eli squealed and ran around the coffee table, once, twice, three times.

They both smiled at his enthusiasm, then Jenna's smile faded.

"What?" Matt asked.

She shook her head.

"Jenna?"

"I feel guilty."

"About what?"

"That I feel happy right now."

"You deserve to feel happy."

"Not when Eli's mother is dead, his father will surely be dead soon, your friend Kyle is in danger and who knows what happened to Marcus."

He pulled her into a hug. "We don't know what the next few days will bring. Enjoying the peaceful moments will help us stay strong during the challenges ahead."

She looked up at him. "How did you become this person?"

"I'm not sure I understand the question."

"You don't freak out about stuff. You're so wise and so…grounded. I've never known a man like you."

"I'm not perfect, Jenna."

"I know," she whispered.

The way she looked up into his eyes…

He leaned forward and kissed her, the connection shooting sparks of energy through his body. This felt so incredible, so normal and right.

Alarm bells went off in his head.

This growing personal connection to Jenna would put her in more danger. It would definitely distract him from doing his job—protecting her and Eli.

He broke the kiss and stepped back. "I shouldn't have done that. I'm sorry."

Disappointment shuttered her eyes.

"That was inappropriate," he added. "Emotional involvement between us will throw me off my game."

"No worries. I was probably giving off signals or something."

"Don't take responsibility for my actions."

Her eyes widened as if he'd insulted her, and then she quickly turned to Eli.

"What are you doing, little man?" She went to him, using the child to derail the conversation.

The kiss. The intense connection growing between them, a connection he suspected had developed in part because of the danger hounding them.

But these feelings, the kiss, none of it was real.

Really, Weller? You sticking with that story?

She pulled a toy out of Eli's bag, and Matt turned on the TV with the remote. Any sounds were preferable to awkward silence. He'd crossed the line.

The little boy burst into giggles. Eli's joy reminded Matt of what he'd been missing: a wife, a family.

Sarah had been right when she said being married to Matt meant raising children as a single parent. He couldn't expect any woman to agree to those terms because, well, no one could love Matt enough to live under that kind of pressure.

He glanced over his shoulder into the parking lot. The same five vehicles that had been parked when he and Jenna arrived were still there. No new cars had pulled in.

Redirecting his attention to the television, he surfed a few channels until he found the news.

And there, filling the screen, was Jenna's face.

He took a few steps closer to the TV.

"We're standing outside of the Cedar River Police Department, where the chief just finished a news conference about a missing child, Eli McFadden…"

Clutching a building block in her hand, Jenna snapped her head around to look at the television. As the reporter continued, Jenna's face drained of color.

"If seen, the Cedar River Police request you call the one eight hundred number at the bottom of your screen. The suspect, Jenna North, is not considered dangerous, but the child has a medical condition and needs to be returned to his family immediately. Back to you, Amy."

"A medical condition?" Jenna glanced at Matt. "Chloe never said anything about a medical condition."

"That type of alert creates a sense of urgency to motivate witnesses to call the police."

"Even more people will be looking for us now."

As if on cue, someone pounded on the cabin door, and Matt drew his weapon.

TEN

Jenna instinctively grabbed Eli. Matthew motioned for her to take the little boy into the bedroom, out of sight.

They both knew the reality of this situation: they were trapped in the cabin with no escape route.

She snatched Eli's diaper bag and rushed into the bedroom.

This was it, the end. Her brain spun with panic. It had to be the authorities coming to take Eli away from her, arrest Jenna for kidnapping and give the child back to his father.

No, that wouldn't happen, because Gary was on the run. So where would this precious little boy end up?

She shut the bedroom door. Eli squirmed against her, wanting to get down and play. She glanced at the closet. Her first instinct was to hide…

"No more hiding," she said softly.

Instead, she put Eli down on the floor with a few toys, and she searched the room for a weapon, something with which to defend herself and Eli.

As she went through the closet, she decided she could use a wire hanger to poke someone in the eye. It would inflict more pain than was necessary, but it would serve the purpose, giving her time to get away.

Could she overpower a thug sent to retrieve her and Eli? If not…

She prayed that Matthew would stop the guy from getting into the bedroom. If he couldn't, Jenna would be ready.

As she untwisted the hanger, she wondered how on earth Billings's men kept finding them. Tracking them to Marcus's cabin made sense because he was Chloe's cousin, but how had they found out about this remote spot? Jenna was using a burner phone, and Matt had disabled his GPS. Maybe Chief Billings had tracked them from the recent phone call using triangulation? No, she'd watched too much TV. A small police department like Cedar River wouldn't have access to such technology, would they?

Eli entertained himself by opening and closing the nightstand drawer, putting his bear inside, then taking him out. Jenna uncoiled two more hangers and folded them together to create a four-pronged weapon. She clutched the hangers in her right hand and pressed her ear to the door, but the wood was too thick to hear much. On one hand, she was relieved she couldn't hear what was going on because that meant no one could hear Eli's squeals of delight each time he'd find Bubba in the nightstand drawer.

On the other hand, her adrenaline pumped with the anticipation of the bedroom door crashing open and a violent encounter between her and one of Chief Billings's men taking place. She stood behind the door.

Waited.

Inhaled slow, deep breaths.

Casting all your care—

A tap on the window made her yelp. She spun around and spotted Marcus waving from the other side of the glass. Rushing across the room, she slid the window open.

"Marcus, how did you—?"

"Later. Hand me the kid."

She hesitated.

"Don't second-guess yourself now, Jenna. The local police are on the other side of the bedroom door questioning Matt, and they're coming in here next to search for you and Eli."

Trust your gut. Patrice had taught her that. Well, Jenna's gut told her Marcus was one of the good guys.

She tossed her weapon on the bed and grabbed Eli and his bear.

Marcus reached out and she passed Eli through

the window. "Bring his bag. Don't leave anything of his behind."

She stuffed Eli's things into the bag and dropped both hers and Eli's bags out the window. She climbed out and landed on the soft snow.

"Close the window," Marcus whispered.

She slid it down, aware of the blue and red lights flashing across the parking lot. Marcus motioned her away from the small cabin.

Jenna couldn't worry about what would happen next.

About what was happening to Matt.

He'd want her to concentrate on keeping herself and the little boy safe.

Marcus led her down a shoveled walkway past four cabins to a clearing at the north end of the property. He opened the back door of an insipid dark sedan and placed Eli into the back seat of the car. Jenna climbed in beside the little boy.

"You don't have a car seat," she said.

"I'm hoping we don't have to go anywhere."

He shut the door behind her. She entertained Eli by offering him a toy truck. Marcus slid behind the wheel and shut the door.

"How did you find us?" she asked.

Marcus glanced over his shoulder. "Planted a tracking device on the kid's overalls. Tried to tell you back at the cabin, but didn't have a chance."

"What happened with the men who took you into custody?"

"I told them you left yesterday. I said if they released me, I'd help them track you down."

She snapped her attention to him.

"It's called being a double agent," Marcus said. "I convinced them I'm an innocent bystander who could care less about my cousin Chloe or Eli. It wasn't hard to believe. Because my work is so all-consuming, I didn't have much contact with my extended family." He handed her a blanket from the front seat.

"Thanks." She tried draping it around Eli's shoulders, but he would have none of it. "Who took you into custody?"

"Said they were federal agents, but I'm not convinced. Their IDs didn't look real, and once they figured out I could be bought, they let me go—well, with a tracker on my phone. They didn't think I'd notice. Idiots."

"So they followed you?"

"Nah, I tucked the phone beneath the front seat of an eighteen wheeler headed south. Anyway, picked up my spare vehicle from a storage facility outside of town and followed you guys here. I heard on the scanner that local authorities were checking out all cabins, resorts, you name it, in Bonner County. I figured once they questioned Matt, they'd move on to the next cabin, and when they're done questioning everyone on-site, they'll check it off the list and head west. After they're gone, the resort will actually be the safest place to hide out for a few days."

"Safe would be nice for a change." Jenna glanced in the direction of their cabin, but couldn't see anything. "Don't you worry that they'll come ask you what you're doing sitting here?"

"They've already asked. Said I'd been driving for twelve hours and needed to catch some sleep. They bought it. They're looking for a couple and a little boy, not a single guy who hasn't shaved in a week."

She wheeled one of Eli's toy trucks across the leather seat. "By the way, Gary found me in the shed."

"What? How?"

"I have no idea. You think he's tracking Eli like you tracked him?"

"I should check the kid's stuff. Hand me his bag."

She passed it to him. "Gary seemed scared. He said he wanted out. That's why they're after Eli, for leverage against him."

"What did that lug nut get himself into this time?" he muttered.

"This time?"

"I did a background check on the guy before Chloe married him. Gary likes to push the envelope. He built his business by breaking into secure IT systems and exposing their vulnerabilities. Maybe he broke into one system too many."

"Or maybe he's involved with the cartel."

"What cartel?"

"Matt thinks there's a connection between Chief Billings and the Guerro drug cartel suspected of laundering money through the foundation."

"Does he have proof?"

"Not yet."

"Too bad. That would put a quick end to all this." He rolled Eli's clothes up one piece at a time and repacked them in the bag. "It's clean."

"How did you track us?"

"Top right button on his overall strap."

Jenna looked closely and saw a small dark disc.

"Cops are headed this way," Marcus said. "Stay down."

Jenna coaxed Eli onto the floor and draped the blanket over herself and Eli. "We're in a fort, Eli," she whispered. The floodlights from the parking lot gave off enough light to illuminate the blanket fort. Eli reached out with a dimpled finger, poked at the blanket and giggled.

Time seemed to drag by as she struggled to keep Eli entertained so he wouldn't cry out for something, such as a bottle, which she didn't have handy.

You can do it, Jenna. You're a natural at this.

She dug into his bag for a new and exciting toy

to entertain him. "What's this?" She pulled out a clear wand with sparkling stars that glittered as they slid from one end to the other. The little boy's eyes lit up.

She steeled herself for the tap on the window from police, demanding to check Marcus's car again.

Casting all your care upon Him; for He careth for you.

At least she knew God cared for Eli, an innocent child.

She used a visualization technique her counselor had taught her after she'd left Anthony. She pictured taking her anxiety and fear and forming it into a snowball, then hurling it toward a tree, where it exploded into pieces. She much preferred the freedom of release to the bondage of anxiety.

As she pointed the star wand up toward the top of their fort, she noticed her trembling hand.

Apparently her visualization didn't totally ease the trepidation in her body.

"Look at those beautiful stars, Eli," she said softly. "Blue and green and red."

Eli grabbed the wand out of her hand and waved it left, then right. As he swung it over his head, he hit the blanket and she suspected they'd lose their cover if she didn't act quickly.

"Eli, look at this." She pulled a pink plastic pig out of his bag and made a soft oinking noise.

Eli giggled and mimicked her. She couldn't help but smile.

She fully embraced this moment, even with danger looming close, and surrendered her worry to God.

"We're clear," Marcus said from the front seat.

Jenna threw back the blanket. "They're gone?"

"They're pulling out of the lot." He slid a device out from beneath the driver's seat and clicked it on. "Let's listen in on the scanner."

"Base, we've cleared the Lazy Shade Resort, over," a voice announced.

"Where to next, over?"

"South to Coeur d'Alene, over."

"Ten-four."

Marcus glanced at Jenna. "Let's get back to the cabin. We'll leave the car here in case we need to make another escape out the bedroom window." He winked.

"Eli's going to wear a cape, like Superman, aren't you, Eli?" She packed up his toys and wrapped the blanket around him. "Ready."

Marcus got out and opened the door for her. She noticed he'd brought the scanner with him so they could continue to monitor police activity. Even though he said police had left the premises, she still found herself peeking between cabins to scan the parking lot for cops.

They made it back to the cabin and reentered the same way they'd left, through the window.

The minute she put Eli down on the floor, he ran back to the nightstand to continue his game of hide-and-seek with Bubba the bear.

The boy was remarkable. If only Jenna could be as unflappable as Eli.

As she headed for the door to the living area, Marcus stepped in front of her.

"Let me go first," he said.

He slipped his gun out of a holster at his belt and cracked open the door. She watched as his eyes darted left and right.

She instinctively went to stand near Eli.

Marcus pushed the door wide, stepped into the living area…

And froze, raising his hands.

The county police officer had asked pointed questions, which Matt answered directly. Then the cop said he needed to search the cabin. Matt held his breath when he pushed open the bedroom door, trying to figure out how to explain Jenna and Eli's presence.

When the cop turned, thanked Matt and left, Matt bolted into the bedroom.

They were gone. Vanished. He rushed to the closet.

Empty.

He looked out the window. No sign of them.

Matt tried coming up with an explanation. She wouldn't have taken Eli away.

Not willingly, at least.

He shoved the window open. Boot prints were visible in the snow. As well as a second set of prints, and both led away from the cabin.

They'd taken her and the child. Matt had failed to protect them.

Panic coursing through his body, he rushed into the living room and grabbed his jacket to go in search of Jenna and Eli.

Then he heard a thump in the next room. Matt stalked silently across the cabin, positioning himself beside the bedroom door.

It creaked open, and a pistol pointed through the doorway into the cabin.

"Drop the gun," Matt said.

The intruder did as ordered and stepped into the living area.

Marcus.

Didn't matter. Matt couldn't trust anyone.

"Take it easy," Marcus said.

"Drop the pack."

Marcus squatted and let it drop off his shoulders. "Matt—"

"Where are Jenna and Eli?" Matthew said.

"We're here," Jenna said, stepping up to the doorway.

He couldn't look at her, not when he needed every ounce of attention to be on Marcus.

"Eli and I are fine," Jenna said. "Marcus kept us safe. What are you—?"

"Go sit at the kitchen table," he ordered Marcus.

The former Navy SEAL did as ordered.

"Jenna, tie Marcus's hands behind his back. There's duct tape in my bag."

"But Matt—"

"Do it."

She hesitated, and then followed Matt's order. The little boy toddled behind her. Noticing the barrel of his gun pointed across the room, Matt felt remorse about Eli witnessing Matt's aggressive stance.

But he had no choice. He needed to keep Jenna safe.

He wasn't going to lose her again.

Jenna led Eli to the sofa and handed him his bear. "Bubba wants to play."

Matt didn't take his eyes off Marcus, who directed his gaze to the floor.

Jenna went to Marcus and tied his hands behind his back. "Sorry," she said softly.

"It's fine. Matt's doing his job."

Standing, she planted her hands on her hips and squared off with Matt. "I don't get it. He's on our side."

"Don't be naive, Jenna. He led the authorities here."

It was the only explanation as to how they'd been found so easily.

"I didn't, Matt, honest," Marcus said.

Jenna wandered closer to Matt. "Then why would he protect me and little Eli?"

"It probably earns him a bigger payout in the end."

"He's Chloe's cousin. Eli's cousin," Jenna argued.

"Then how did the police know to check this resort for us?"

"It was a random check," Marcus argued.

"Because you knew we were here." Matt leaned against the wall and lowered his gun. "How did you know our location?"

"He put a tracker on Eli's overalls," Jenna said.

"Making sure you don't lose your payday, huh, Marcus?"

"There is no amount of money worth Eli's life," the man argued.

"Save it. I found out your bank account has a little over a hundred-dollar balance, and you've got a balloon payment due on your cabin next month."

Marcus didn't say anything at first. Matt supposed that was because it was hard to argue with the truth.

"I've got an explanation if you're willing to listen," Marcus said.

Matt nodded, not that he'd believe the man's lies.

"I keep most of my money offshore to protect my clients' identities," Marcus explained. "I can log in on my phone and show you my accounts. I've got over three hundred thousand in my Cayman account."

"You have an answer for everything, don't you?" Matt said.

"Plus, the job I recently completed is going to deposit ten grand into my US bank account."

Matt heard the man's words, but his explanation didn't ease the distrust in his heart.

"What can I do to convince you I'm on your side?"

"I believe him," Jenna said.

Matt glanced at her innocent and trusting expression. How could she be so naive after everything that had happened to them?

"Marcus said they let him go because he agreed to be a double agent," she said.

Matt snapped his attention to Marcus.

"He's pretending to work for them so he can help us protect Eli," Jenna continued.

"You're too trusting," he ground out, adrenaline still pulsing through his body.

"If he'd wanted to turn me over to Billings, he would have taken us away."

"But he didn't, and now they know where we are. We're easy targets," Matt said.

"Matt—" Marcus began.

"I'm not talking to you," Matt interrupted him.

"Marcus said we'd be safe here because police checked the premises and didn't find us, so there's no reason for them to come back," Jenna said. "We listened to the scanner. They're headed south."

Matt couldn't take his eyes off Marcus, trying to logically assess the situation. What Jenna was saying made sense. Marcus could have left with Jenna and Eli.

But he hadn't. He'd brought them back inside.

To Matt.

Because being here, in a cabin that had been checked and cleared, was the safest place for them to hide.

It dawned on him that Jenna was being the grounded one, while Matt orbited in crazy world.

Because he cared so much about Jenna. Were his feelings making him paranoid and distrustful when he didn't need to be?

"May I speak?" Marcus asked.

Matt nodded.

"I'll admit I agreed to be their spy to find you guys and expose your location. I could have done that just now, but I didn't. Matt, I'd never do anything that would put Eli in jeopardy. You've gotta believe me."

Silence permeated the room as Matt studied the man tied to a chair. Eli ran up to Jenna and raised his arms.

"What's your story, little man?" she said, picking him up.

Protect them. You have to protect them.

"We need to pack up and get out of here," Matt said.

"That's a bad move—"

"Quiet," Matt interrupted Marcus.

"Matthew?" Jenna said tentatively.

He glanced at her as she bounced little Eli in her arms.

"Why not listen to the scanner to see if it's safe to leave?" She went to Marcus's bag, pulled out a scanner and walked it over to Matt.

He holstered his weapon and clicked it on.

For the next few minutes they listened to the activity of local law enforcement. Cops were spread out everywhere. Of course they were, because a child's life was at stake—a child with a phantom medical condition.

Leaving the resort and fleeing on any surrounding roads would be risky.

And extremely dangerous.

As Matt fought to find clarity, he struggled against the panic that had blinded him when he'd opened the bedroom door and they were gone.

"My gut tells me staying here is the best choice," Jenna said.

Her gut told her. This woman who'd been abused by her former husband, chased by thugs for the past few days and survived more than one dangerous situation was relying on instinct. She was able to trust her gut, while Matt's was a tangled mess.

Thinking critically, as an agent without a personal agenda, Matt catalogued the facts in his mind—Marcus's background check had come up clean. Marcus could have turned Jenna over to Billings's men—twice now—but he hadn't.

Jenna and Eli were safe. They were here, right in front of him.

Because Marcus had protected them.

"You can leave me tied up if you want," Marcus said. "I'm okay with that."

Matt glanced from Jenna to Marcus and back to Jenna. They both looked at him like he was a little insane, maybe a lot insane, and with good reason. Matt's perspective had been blown apart.

He was falling in love with Jenna North, which put both Jenna and Eli at risk.

"Look," Marcus began. "Chloe didn't have an easy childhood. My aunt and uncle were mean drunks. I saw what was going on, but I was just a kid. Chloe suffered her share of abuse and I couldn't protect her. I'd really like to help protect her son."

It was a reasonable request, an honorable request, from a man who loved his family.

Matt started to come down from his adrenaline rush and realized his paranoia stemmed from the feeling that someone close to them was feeding information to the other side, setting up Matt, Eli and Jenna to be snared like animals in a trap.

As he studied Marcus, the sounds of a playful little boy drifted across the cabin. A boy who was happy and safe.

Jenna touched Matt's arm. He couldn't look at her. He'd just lost his concentration, his professionalism. This time it didn't threaten anything, didn't put them at risk.

But next time?

Bottom line—the thought of losing Jenna had destroyed his ability to think clearly.

You're in big trouble, Weller.

When she squeezed his arm, he glanced into her caring green eyes.

"What do you think?" she asked.

Voices echoed from the scanner and it was obvious that the county officers were heading away from the Lazy Shade Resort, in both directions. Assuming the thugs who'd been after Jenna, Matt and Eli were also listening to the scanner, and using that information to decide where to look next, Matt decided that staying put was a safe choice, at least for now.

He also admitted he was overreacting in regards to Marcus, whose background check had portrayed him as a dedicated soldier who'd earned a medal for valor in combat. What more did Matt want?

He crossed the cabin, pulled out his knife and cut Marcus's hands free. "Sorry."

"No problem. I appreciate how much you care about Eli."

More like how much Matt cared about Jenna. Not good. He had to…

What? Stop caring about her? That ship had sailed and wasn't coming back to port. Instead, he had to make a responsible decision: find a replacement guardian, someone who'd have the necessary perspective to protect Jenna, not put her at greater risk.

Jenna studied him with an odd expression, as if she were trying to read his thoughts. Matt turned to the counter to make coffee.

"I'm not sure what the plan is, but I've got a tablet in my bag if that'll help," Marcus said.

"Getting Gary to testify against the cartel would be the biggest help," Matt said.

"That weasel?" Marcus went to retrieve his tablet. "Not likely."

"What do you mean?" Matt asked, scooping grounds into the coffee maker.

"I did surveillance on Gary before Chloe married him." Marcus sat at the kitchen table with his tablet.

Jenna continued to play with Eli, but her eyes were on Matt.

"As I told Jenna," Marcus started, "Gary would hack into IT systems to prove his talent as a tech specialist. The companies he broke into were either so grateful that they hired him as a consultant, or in some cases they threatened to take legal action."

Matt turned to Marcus. "Were charges ever brought against him? Because we never found any."

"Nope. He only exposed his identity to companies that had something to lose."

"I don't understand."

"Companies that were involved in questionable activity, maybe even criminal activity. Basically Gary would breach their system, they'd threaten to bring charges and he'd threaten to expose them. Then they'd back off."

"That's a good way to make enemies," Matt said.

"You're thinking this may not be related to the cartel's money laundering?"

"Perhaps, except that Gary's exact words were, *There is no getting out*," Matt said. "That sounds like the cartel."

"Although he didn't come out and admit it," Jenna offered.

"Maybe he didn't want to incriminate himself?" Marcus suggested.

"It would help to have access to Gary's emails," Matt said.

"I know a guy—"

"We need to keep this legal," Matt interrupted Marcus. "I'll contact my IT guy at the agency."

"Marcus, did you tell Chloe about Gary hacking into secure systems?" Jenna asked.

"She didn't want to hear it. She was so in love,

kept saying how her life was finally working out and she'd found a kind man to take care of her, someone who was the opposite of her dad. She was angry with me for trying to ruin her happily-ever-after and, well, we didn't talk much after that."

"She was in love with the idea of love and security," Jenna said softly.

Matt sensed she was speaking from experience.

"Some would say Gary was pretty harmless, just manipulative for a buck," Marcus added.

Jenna handed Eli a toy. "Not so harmless if his work put his family at risk."

"True," Marcus agreed.

Matt joined Marcus at the table, careful to avoid Jenna's scrutiny. How was he going to do this? How was he going to leave her and Eli in someone else's care and not share his reasons for the decision? Because he knew if he told her of his plan, she'd push back.

He sensed she was feeling it too, this pull between them.

"You okay?" she said with a questioning frown.

She knew something was up, and somehow he had to distract her from figuring out his next move.

"I'll be better once we put an end to this thing."

They spent the next day going through online files, even Jenna's work files, to see if the flow of money was going through her foundation fund. She certainly hoped not. The thought of somehow being a party to the cartel's money laundering sent a shudder down her spine. Is that why the big donations had come in? Because they were being funneled from the cartel?

While she took care of Eli, either Matt or Marcus would keep an eye out the window, as the other took the lead on digging into the case via the tablet.

Jenna stretched out on the bed beside Eli for his afternoon nap. As she lay there, humming the little boy to sleep, Matthew's words taunted her:

I'll be better once we put an end to this thing.

So would Jenna, although she admitted she didn't want her time with Matt to come to an end. How dysfunctional was that? He was just doing his job, that's all.

Yet last night he'd seemed irrational about Marcus being a threat. She wasn't sure she'd be able to talk him out of his dark place. Ironic that she'd been the grounded one in that situation.

Ironic and refreshing. Jenna was learning to cope with dire situations more quickly than ever before. She no longer felt the need to run every time things got hard.

With a sigh, she studied the ceiling and pictured an easier life where she and Matt went for pizza, took Eli sledding, or even…attended church.

Wow, where had that thought come from?

She remembered him talking about how God had touched her life, how He brought the women of Gloria's Guardians to her, how she'd developed strength through tragedy.

Matt's words had resonated deep within Jenna. Somehow this man had peeled away the resentment encapsulating her heart, the anger she clung to against a God who never seemed to listen.

Yet hadn't He? After everything she'd been through these past few days, Eli was safe. And Jenna was still safe too, even with a police bulletin out on her.

She silently thanked God.

As night darkened the cabin, Eli awoke in an irritable mood. She completely understood since she wasn't one to wake up with a grin on her face most mornings either. She changed him, gave him his bear and went into the living room, where Marcus sat at the kitchen table, studying his tablet, and Matthew kept watch out the window.

"How'd you sleep?" Marcus asked.

Matthew glanced at Jenna and offered a strained smile, but didn't say anything.

"Eli slept pretty well, didn't you, little dude?" she said. He rubbed his cheek with his bear and leaned against her shoulder.

"Wish I could say we've made progress," Marcus said. "But even the FBI tech can't crack Gary's code and back doors to his files."

"So we're no better off than we were a few hours ago," Jenna said, heading into the kitchen.

"Jenna?" Matthew said.

She turned to him.

"We'll figure it out."

A sudden crash sounded from the bedroom.

"Stay here," Matt ordered, drawing his firearm.

He rushed across the cabin and disappeared into the bedroom just as something hurled through the living room window, shattering the glass.

"Close your eyes!" Marcus shouted.

ELEVEN

Clutching Eli, Jenna dropped to the floor and shielded his face. Taking purposeful deep breaths, she was able to calm her racing heart and focus on protecting the little boy.

The front door slammed open with a crash.

"Get on the ground!" a man shouted.

The police? No, but they'd already been here, Marcus said—

Another crash was followed by a grunt.

Something was flashing behind her eyelids, probably a flash bomb, which is why Marcus had yelled to keep her eyes closed.

Suddenly a firm hand gripped her arm.

"Let him go!" a man shouted.

She clenched her jaw, knowing what was coming next and not caring. Nothing would make her release Eli.

Something smacked her in the head. She saw stars. But still wouldn't let go.

The child wailed into her ear.

"She won't let go of the kid!"

"Kill him!"

Kill Eli?

The man jerked back and released her. She guessed Marcus had come to her aid.

Clicking into protective mode, she opened the cabinet door beneath the sink and did a hand search for something she could use against her attacker. Then she got an even better idea. With a swipe of her hand, she cleared everything out from under the sink.

Against his protests, she slid Eli into the cabinet and shut the door. Again, without opening her eyes, she felt around for a bottle of something she'd taken out of the cabinet. She opened one and sniffed. A pine-scented disinfectant. Perfect.

She turned her back to the struggle going on behind her and pretended to still be holding Eli.

Men's grunts echoed across the cabin.

The flashing stopped.

"Bedroom clear!" a man shouted.

The bedroom? Where Matt had gone to check out the sound of a breaking window?

"Get 'em!" the other guy shouted, but it sounded like he was still tangling with Marcus.

She waited. Took a deep breath.

Tuned in to her highly sensitized instincts honed from years of anticipating when Anthony was coming for her.

She sensed the assailant was getting close.

And the next moment he pinched her arm and yanked her back.

In one fluid movement, she spun around and jerked the open bottle of disinfectant upward, making sure to keep her eyes closed in case of backsplash.

The guy cried out. His gun went off, causing her ears to ring.

"I can't see!" the man shouted and stumbled back against the kitchen table.

Behind her, Eli screamed from his safe hiding spot.

"Stupid cow!" the other guy said.

He was no longer fighting with Marcus. No, he was headed her way.

Deep breath, deep breath.

She curled into herself, clutching the bottle.

Cracked her eyes open.

He grabbed her and she jerked the bottle upward, but he yanked it out of her hand. She scrambled to get away and he grabbed her hair.

She screamed. Someone dove at the man...

Matthew.

He flung the attacker across the kitchen table. The gun flew out of his hands and slid across the floor. Eli pushed against the doors beneath the sink.

Jenna slammed her foot against the cabinet to keep Eli safe, and splayed her hands across the vinyl floor to grab the gun. Could she really shoot someone? Yes, if it meant saving her life.

Eli's life.

Matthew's life.

Her fingers wrapped around cold steel. With a firm grip on the gun, she scooted back to her protective position against the cabinet where Eli's muted cries echoed.

Casting all your care on Him...

She aimed the gun, ready to shoot.

Marcus lay unconscious a few feet away. The thug she'd nailed with the disinfectant had disappeared, probably into the bathroom to wash out his eyes.

Matthew and the other attacker punched and kicked, stumbling back toward the kitchen. That's when she spotted the blood on Matthew's shirt.

They hit the floor and rolled, getting dangerously close to slamming into Jenna. She held her position.

Should she do it now? Shoot the attacker?

What if she missed and shot Matthew by accident?

They rolled again. Knocked over a chair. The attacker pinned Matthew, pummeling his fist into the bullet wound. Matthew cried out and rolled away. The attacker turned to Jenna.

She pulled the trigger.

The guy stumbled backward, just for a second. Then he lunged and ripped the gun out of her hand before she could fire again. He'd obviously been wearing a protective vest.

He pulled her to her feet.

She stomped on the top of his foot and jerked her fingers up to poke him in the eyes.

He caught her wrist. His wicked eyes glowed with delight. He grabbed her neck with his firm hand.

She kicked, swung her arms.

Just as stars flitted across her vision, a chair smashed against the side of the guy's head and he released her.

Matthew. He was up again, fighting to save her life.

Jenna skirted away just as Eli flung open the cabinet and tumbled onto the floor. She grabbed the little boy and held him close. Rocking him back and forth, she whispered, "It's okay, sweet boy. It's okay." Even though she knew it wasn't.

Please, God, help us.

"Matt, stop!" Marcus shouted.

Jenna opened her eyes and spotted Matthew, swinging a chair leg at the attacker over and over again, a wild expression pinching his forehead. She almost didn't recognize him.

"Matt!" Marcus tried grabbing the wooden weapon out of his hands, but Matt yanked it away. "Stop! You're going to kill him!"

Hooked by fury, he was being pulled further into the darkness.

Because the man he was beating senseless had tried to strangle Jenna to death.

She stood and cupped Eli's head against her shoulder. Stepping closer to the violent scene, she said firmly, "Matthew."

He hesitated and looked at her with empty blue eyes.

"It's okay. You can stop now. We're all okay."

He blinked, as if his brain had gone offline, shut down. He glanced at the guy on the floor.

"He's neutralized," Marcus confirmed.

"What about the other guy?" she asked.

A car door slammed outside and an engine turned over.

"He probably didn't want any of this." Marcus nodded at the unconscious man on the floor. "Hate to state the obvious, but we've got to get outta here."

Matthew didn't move at first, still staring at the beaten man.

"You guys take my car," Marcus said. "I'll drive your truck in case they're looking for it."

"What about Matthew's gunshot wound?" Jenna said.

"I'm fine." He stood, wavered slightly and avoided eye contact. "Let's move."

Matthew wasn't fine, and Jenna had to do something to help him. He'd sacrificed himself so many times for her.

As she cast a quick glance at her semiconscious passenger, guilt taunted her. He'd wanted to go to the authorities from day one, to follow proper channels, but her posttrauma issues made her suspicious, especially of law enforcement, and even of Matthew. And now this man couldn't get proper medical attention because they needed to keep moving.

After a few hours in the car, Eli started squirming and she decided to pick up food. A little sustenance would help her think clearly and map out their next steps.

Catching her reflection in the rearview, she realized she looked different from her former self.

Nor did she feel like the old Jenna, the weak Jenna who cowered from bullies. A flash of the scene in the cabin replayed in her mind: flinging disinfectant, kicking the man's leg…shooting him in the chest.

She was stronger now, more confident. Even with police and cartel thugs looking for her and Eli, she wasn't afraid.

She was determined.

Just as Matthew had been determined to save her life ever since the night he'd found her fleeing the community center. They'd grown close as they escaped danger, danger that almost drove him to commit murder on her behalf. She'd never forget the lost look in his eyes as he hovered over the attacker, gripping the chair leg. He would have continued hitting him, but somehow she'd pierced his adrenaline trance and had gotten through to him. His expression of rage eased into confusion and then…remorse.

In Jenna's opinion, he had nothing to be sorry about. Jenna would have done the same thing, if she'd had the physical strength, to save Matt's life.

That's what you did for the people you loved.

Love? Was that even realistic considering how they'd met?

She couldn't think about that now. Her biggest concern had to be keeping the three of them safe.

Staying under the speed limit so as not to draw unwanted attention from authorities, she mentally prioritized her goals: keep Eli safe. And don't let Matthew die.

She glanced at her passenger yet again. Matt was still semiconscious. He couldn't offer suggestions or advice about what to do next.

She was on her own and in charge of protecting the two people she cared about most in this world. She could do this and she knew how, only Matthew probably wouldn't approve.

A few minutes later she pulled off the expressway to get food. And make the call.

"What…why are we stopped?" he asked, blinking his eyes open.

"I'm picking up food. May I borrow your phone?"

He nodded and handed it to her.

"Can you stay here and protect Eli?" she said.

"Yeah," he replied groggily. "Sure."

"I'll leave the keys in case you need to get out of here quick."

"I'm not going anywhere without you."

"Eli's safety comes first, remember?"

He nodded.

Eli's safety. The sweet boy had been exposed to way too much violence. He kicked his little feet and reached for Jenna.

"Hang on, buddy," she said. She went into the back seat and made sure he had his pacifier and bear. "Be right back."

A new kind of strength surged through her. She was the protector now, and she would succeed.

She tucked her hair into a knit cap and crossed the parking lot. A plan had clearly formed in her mind. She hesitated outside the restaurant and made her first call.

"Hello?" Patricc answered.

"It's Jenna."

"Oh, my friend, I've been worried about you."

"I need a favor. It's a big ask, so don't feel bad about saying no."

"Go on."

"Do you have anyone staying with you?"

"Not at present, no."

"Not Emily?"

"The Millers decided to give her another chance."

Jenna smiled to herself. "Good, that's good."

"How can I help?"

"My friend's little boy is still in danger. He needs a safe place to stay while I sort things out."

"Of course he's welcome here."

"It could be dangerous. Bad men are after him."

"All the more reason for the Guardians to protect him. How far away are you?"

"I'm guessing about four hours. I have to make a stop first."

"Want me to meet you halfway?"

"No, but let's not meet at your place. I don't want to expose the network."

"How about Remington's Pancake House?"

"Too public. There's the old gray barn historic site just outside of Post Falls. You know it?"

"No, but I'll plug it into my GPS and find it."

"I'll text you when I'm half an hour out."

"Sounds good."

With renewed hope, Jenna went into the restaurant and stepped up to the counter to order food.

"May I help you?" a teenager behind the counter asked.

"Sure, I'll have three burgers with fries and a chocolate shake."

"Everything on the burgers?"

"Ketchup and mustard only. Hey, have you seen a man with three little kids in Broncos gear?"

"Um…"

"You can't miss him. He's super tall."

"No, sorry."

"Okay, thanks."

"Three burgers and large fries," the cashier repeated.

"Oh, and two orders of chicken tenders." Jenna sighed. "I'd be in big trouble if I forget the tenders. With honey and ranch sauce."

"Sounds good."

Jenna paid and stepped aside for the next customer. Ordering a lot of food and asking about a man with three children gave the illusion she was with a group, not just one man and a child.

She mentally repeated her goals once more: *keep Eli safe*. Check. She would place him safely and anonymously with Patrice.

Don't let Matthew die. There was only one way to accomplish that goal.

A few minutes later, she collected two bags of food and headed for the car. She glanced through the back window, and her breath caught. She didn't see Matthew in the passenger seat. Jogging across the lot, she looked through the driver's side window.

Matthew lay unconscious on the front seat. She flung open the back door and placed the food beside Eli, then handed him a French fry to nibble on. He squealed and sucked on the fry.

She opened the front door. "Matthew?" She felt for a pulse. Weak, but steady.

Propping him up against the passenger door,

she climbed into the car. Upon closer inspection, she saw that blood had soaked through the dressing Marcus had applied to Matthew's gunshot wound.

"You're gonna be okay," she whispered and pulled out of the parking lot.

"Jenna," Matt said on a gasp, opening his eyes.

Surrounded by pale-colored walls, he fought the confusion pickling his brain.

"Matt."

He turned to the source of the sound and was looking at his friend, Officer Kyle Armstrong.

"Kyle?" he croaked, his voice weak. Matt shifted, and pain seared down his arm to his fingertips. Right, he'd taken a bullet in the shoulder at the cabin.

"We're here in an official capacity."

"Where's Jenna?" Matt asked.

"That's what you're going to tell us." Chief Billings stepped into view. Matt realized his uninjured arm was cuffed to the bed.

"You're under arrest for kidnapping," Billings said.

"Kidnapping?"

"We thought Jenna North kidnapped the child, but it's obvious you kidnapped both the woman and child and held them hostage. What for, money?" Billings said. "What did Gary McFadden promise you? And where can we find him?"

"I don't know."

"Not good enough," Billings said. "There's a warrant out on Gary McFadden for embezzlement. He's been diverting funds from the Broadlake Foundation into offshore accounts. We suspect his wife is going to meet up with her husband in another country."

Matt clenched his jaw. They both knew Gary's wife was dead, and the killer was standing here spewing lies.

"You must have found out about their little side business and decided the best way to get some of that money was to kidnap the child," Billings continued.

Matt didn't argue or explain himself. There was no sense losing energy by fighting well-crafted lies.

"But for the McFaddens to leave their little boy behind?" Billings said. "In the care of an unstable woman like Jenna North? How cruel. It wouldn't surprise me if both the woman and child came to a tragic end."

Matt fisted his cuffed hand.

"What was your role in this?" Kyle questioned. "Were you Jenna North's bodyguard? Hired to protect the child until he could be reunited with his parents?"

"Lawyer," Matt said.

Billings's eye twitched. Kyle shook his head in disappointment.

Billings stepped around to the other side of the bed and analyzed Matt's dressing. "I was shot once. In the thigh. Hurt like a red-hot poker searing into my skin."

Matt glared at Billings, waiting.

"I wonder if it hurts as bad in the shoulder as it did in the leg?" He reached out.

"Chief," Kyle said, eyeing his phone. "A witness spotted the vehicle heading east on I-90."

Billings didn't shift away, his fingers mere inches from Matt's wound.

"Chief, we should be there to help bring her in," Kyle prompted.

She? Jenna? They'd located her?

"Leave him cuffed to the bed," Billings said.

"Yes, sir."

Billings retreated and started for the door.

"Jeremiah, huh?" Leaning closer to Matt with a closed fist against the bed for support, Kyle said, "You're no longer my family."

Shame coursed through Matt, then panic. His friend hadn't understood the meaning of the scripture reference. He didn't know Billings was a threat, and Kyle's life was in danger because of his friendship with Matt.

Kyle quickly turned and marched out.

Billings cracked a victorious smile. "We'll be back."

They disappeared into the hallway.

With a sigh of frustration, Matt fought the helplessness coursing through him. He shifted slightly. And felt something cool beside his cuffed wrist.

The key to the cuffs.

Adrenaline kept Jenna's mind sharp. She was only twenty minutes away from the barn and had texted Patrice that she was close.

She hadn't wanted to involve Patrice, but she was out of options. She surely wasn't going to turn herself and Eli in to the police, not with the lies being broadcast about her. Eli would end up in Child Protective Services with strangers who could very well have connections to the cartel.

The boy's father had said they were after Eli for leverage against Gary, and Jenna would make sure they wouldn't get anywhere near the child.

Jenna had taken charge.

She'd left Matthew at the hospital without his gun because she remembered him saying before that it would alarm staff. So she locked it in the glove box. Eli would stay with Patrice, and Jenna was driving Marcus's car that no one could trace back to her.

She'd found Agent Barnes's number from Matthew's cell phone and left the agent a message about where she'd taken Matthew for medical care. She said she would turn herself in to authorities once she'd found a safe place for little Eli.

It was time to stop running.

She'd never give up Eli's location, not until the case was resolved and she knew the child was safe. That goal would no doubt result in her being arrested, tried and convicted for any number of federal crimes.

She didn't care. All that mattered was Eli's safety.

Jenna finally felt like the person Chloe had hoped she was: a woman who wouldn't back down or be intimidated.

A friend who wouldn't let anything happen to Chloe's child.

Eli squawked from the back seat.

"What's up? You lose your Bubba? We're almost there, baby boy," Jenna said.

She turned right onto the dark drive leading to the abandoned farmhouse. As she got closer, she looked for Patrice's car. She'd probably parked out of view in case a local patrolman cruised by on his or her shift.

A light blinked from inside the barn. Jenna sighed with relief. Patrice was there, waiting.

All would be well.

She parked in back, beside Patrice's SUV, and grabbed Eli out of his car seat. Handing him the white bear, she headed for the barn.

"You ready to meet my friend? You're going to

like her." Jenna kissed his forehead and stepped inside the barn. "Patrice?"

A flashlight clicked on, blinding her. "She's dead."

TWELVE

Matt uncuffed himself and went to the closet, half expecting his clothes to be missing. Instead, he found a plastic bag with jeans and a clean shirt.

"Thanks, Kyle," he whispered and got dressed.

As he was slipping on his boots, a nurse entered the room. "What are you doing out of bed?"

"Had to use the washroom."

"You had to get dressed to do that?" With a raised eyebrow, she said, "Do I need to call security?"

"I'm FBI, working undercover."

"Sure you are."

He sighed. "Ma'am, I don't know how to convince you, but my case has gone south and I'm afraid a young woman and a child might be killed if I don't get to them."

The middle-aged nurse studied Matt. He held her gaze, hoping she'd read truth in his eyes.

"I'll be back in thirty minutes to check your vitals," she said.

She was giving him notice. He had half an hour to get as far away as he could.

There was only one choice to be made: he needed the resources of the FBI. Even if he wasn't sure whom he could trust, he had to start somewhere.

He had to find Jenna.

Searching his pockets, he realized his phone was missing. He vaguely remembered Jenna asking to borrow it, which meant he could have work track her location. He hoped. He prayed.

Keeping his head down, he exited the hospital without incident and walked north, toward a convenience store lit up in the distance. He had to call in, report to his supervisor and ask Bob for help in tracking Jenna.

A car pulled up beside him and the passenger window rolled down.

"Get in," Bob said from behind the wheel.

"How did you—?"

"Jenna North called me."

"You have her in custody?"

"Not yet."

"We've gotta find her, they're—"

"You really want to have this conversation out here?" Bob said.

Matt got into the car. They pulled away, quiet for a few minutes.

"The Guerro case is blown," Bob said. "All the money's gone, and someone with major tech skills went in and made it look like Jenna North disappeared with the funds."

"Gary," Matt muttered. "No, that makes no sense. He said the cartel was after him, that he'd developed the scheme and wanted out."

"Maybe he found his own way out by pinning it on Jenna. Pragge is out of his mind that the case is in shambles."

"Does he know you're here?"

"Are you kidding? I don't want to lose my job, and you're his least favorite person right now."

"We need to find Jenna," Matt said.

"How do you suggest we do that?" Bob asked.

"She has my phone. Let's get someone at work to ping it for us."

But twenty minutes later, they were unable to get a location on Matt's phone. Had she ditched it because she didn't want to be tracked?

Jenna was out there, alone, with no one to turn to.

"Patrice," he said.

"Who?"

"A woman who helped Jenna before when she escaped her abusive husband."

Matt contacted Nancy Miller and asked for Patrice's phone number. From there, Matt took a chance that Patrice still used a landline.

She did, and they were able to ascertain Patrice's address.

Going to Patrice made the most sense, since

Jenna had been abandoned by Marcus and had given up on Matt's ability to protect her.

Regret tore through him. Exposing Patrice could jeopardize the Guardians, something Jenna was adamant she didn't want to do.

"I need a favor," Matt said to Bob.

"Another one?" Bob teased.

"Don't share Patrice's location with anyone else."

"Why, what's she into?"

"Helping people."

"Sounds noble. I wouldn't want to mess with that."

"Thanks."

A few hours later they pulled up in front of the house. The living room was lit up and the porch light glowed, as if to welcome visitors.

They approached the house and hesitated.

The front door was ajar.

Bob withdrew his firearm. When he realized Matt didn't have his gun, Bob pulled a second one from an ankle holster and offered it to him. He motioned that he was going around to the back of the house. Matt nodded and, gun in hand, toed the front door open.

The living room had been tossed, as if someone had been looking for something. Furniture was tipped over, a ceramic lamp lay in pieces on the floor and cabinet drawers were pulled out, papers strewn across the rug. He checked each room carefully, making it to the back of the house. As he stepped out on the back porch, Bob came around and joined him.

"It's clear," Matt said.

"Clear out here too." He holstered his gun and peeked into the back window. "What happened?"

Matt shook his head, unable to speak, to find words to state the obvious: They'd found and taken Patrice, Jenna and Eli.

He was too late.

He'd failed to protect them.

Why, Jenna, why did you leave me at the hospital?

Because she'd seen his violent side and knew he was capable of beating a man to death. A traumatized and gentle woman like Jenna North couldn't be around that kind of darkness.

"What do we do now?" Bob asked.

"Find Jenna."

"Over my dead body," a woman said behind Matt.

Bob reached for his weapon.

"Don't even," the woman threatened. "Let me see your hands."

"Ma'am, we're FBI agents," Bob said.

"I fell for that once already. Drop your weapons!"

This had to be…

"Patrice?" Matt said, placing his gun on the ground and turning to her.

The middle-aged woman aimed a shotgun at his chest. Her lip was bloody and a bruise was forming on her cheek.

"What happened?" he asked.

"I survived my fall over the cliff, no thanks to your friends."

"What friends?"

"Two guys who claimed to be cops. Cops don't threaten innocent people, and they surely don't hit 'em."

"I'm sorry that they hurt you."

"Hurt me? They threatened to kill me unless I told them where Jenna was. Well, I escaped and slid down the ravine where they couldn't find me."

"You're a strong woman. An inspiration to Jenna."

"Go on, get outta here." She motioned with her shotgun.

He had to convince her he was one of the good guys. "I can prove I'm here to help Jenna."

"One…two…" she counted.

Matt put his hand up to prevent Bob from withdrawing his gun in self-defense.

He nodded at Patrice. "Jenna and I spent a lot of time together. We grew very close. She told me about her ex-husband, and how Gloria's Guardians came to her rescue. She was able to protect a little boy this week thanks to you."

"Three…four—"

"Wait." Matt extended a calming hand. "Her ring, her silver braided ring. You gave it to her as a reminder that you and the Guardians are always there for her, that God's always there. Please, you've got to help me find her."

She lowered the weapon. "You're really him?"

Matt nodded.

"And we're really federal agents," Bob snapped.

"Do you know where she is?" Matt asked Patrice.

"I know where she was going. If they took my car, they do too."

Jenna turned to flee the barn. And was immediately blocked by a tall, broad-shouldered man.

"Nah-uh," he said.

She clung tighter to Eli and looked into the eyes of a killer, the husky, broad-shouldered guy who'd been with Chief Billings the night of Chloe's death.

It was over.

No, I will not accept that.

"Where's Patrice?" she said sharply to the thug.

"I told you, dead," a voice said behind her.

She spun around and a lantern clicked on, illuminating the other side of the barn and…

Chief Billings.

As he sauntered toward her, Jenna's pulse pounded into her throat.

"You're a real pain, ya know that?" Billings said.

"What did you expect me to do? Turn this innocent child over to a killer?"

"Me?" He stopped mere inches from her. "A killer? No, I'm the Cedar River police chief, who found the suspect that embezzled money from the Broadlake Foundation and then kidnapped a child because she'd lost her own."

Jenna held her breath. How could he know about Joey?

"I'll take the child." Billings reached out for Eli.

Jenna turned away from him.

"You can't take him where you're going," Billings said.

"You'll never be able to prove any of this in a court of law."

"I won't have to."

"Hello, Anna."

She gasped. It was Anthony's voice.

Her former husband stepped out of the shadows and offered a menacing smile. "I've missed you."

Her first instinct was to cower. Her second instinct was to fight.

"Shouldn't you still be in jail?" she snapped.

"Early release for good behavior." He winked.

"More like you paid somebody off."

"My, my, you've developed quite the attitude," Anthony said. "I can fix that."

She'd like to see him try.

"I'm sure the loving couple would like some time alone," Billings said and reached for Eli.

Once again she turned away.

"You're being ridiculous," Billings said. "I'd never hurt a kid."

"Then why do you want him?"

"To draw Gary out of hiding. He's made a mess of things."

"You mean the cartel?"

Billings's eyes flared. "Anthony, I'm relying on you to make this disappear."

The tall thug grabbed her shoulders and yanked her back against his chest. Eli wailed.

"Look at that, she and the child have bonded," Anthony said.

She held on as long as she could, but Billings was too strong. He ripped Eli out of her arms.

Then Anthony laughed.

Eli cried, reaching out for her.

Rage consumed her, followed by something even stronger.

Protect Eli.

In a blind fury, she kneed the tall guy in the crotch, ripped the gun out of his hand and smacked it against the side of his head. He stumbled backward. She spun around just as Anthony was about to grab her.

With a quick motion, she broke his nose with the gun, and he cried out in pain.

She aimed the weapon at Billings…who was pointing his gun at Eli. "Put it down."

Now what? If she relinquished her weapon, she was dead. If she didn't, Eli was dead.

She put out her free hand in surrender. And spotted Anthony charging in her direction. "I'm gonna kill you!"

She aimed the gun and fired. He fell to the ground, gripping his shoulder.

"*You* will never hurt *me* again," she said.

She glanced at Billings, who seemed surprised that she'd actually shot Anthony.

"Add attempted murder to the charges," Billings said.

"Let him go!" Gary cried.

Billings spun around and fired a shot into the darkness.

Eli screamed and kicked, making it impossible for Billings to get off a straight shot. He put Eli down and the boy toddled off. Jenna dove to grab him.

Gary rushed Billings.

A shot rang out. Then another.

Jenna backed up toward the exit.

"Get back here!" Anthony shouted, coming after her.

She aimed the gun…

But before she could squeeze the trigger, another shot rang out.

Anthony collapsed mere inches from her. She stared at him, unable to move.

"You're okay," Matthew said. He placed firm hands on her shoulders. She stood there, staring down the barrel of her gun at Anthony's motionless body.

Matthew reached around and slid the gun out of her hand. "Let it go."

She did, but she couldn't look away. Matthew kneeled to check Anthony's pulse. He glanced at Jenna and shook his head.

Her former husband was dead.

Matthew stood and pulled Jenna against his chest. He held her tight, with Eli between them, stroking her hair.

"You're under arrest!" a voice shouted behind her.

Patrice touched Jenna's arm and offered a nod.

"You're okay?" Jenna asked, happy to see her friend.

"I'm tough, remember?"

Only then did Jenna see Eli's father, Gary, motionless on the ground, and a second agent cuffing Chief Billings.

"You have the right to remain silent..." the agent said to Billings.

"Eli... Eli," Gary croaked.

Matthew extended his arm, as if offering to take Eli to his father.

"I can do it," Jenna said. Matthew and Patrice escorted Jenna over to Gary. "Can you cover up his wound?" she asked Matthew.

He took off his jacket and draped it over Gary's stomach, where he'd been hit.

"Ambulance is on the way," the other agent said.

Holding Eli, Jenna kneeled beside the little boy's father.

"Eli." Gary smiled and reached out to touch Eli's cheek. Eli turned away.

"He's scared," Jenna said. "Lots of loud noises, right, buddy?"

"Did you sct up Jenna to take the fall for the money laundering?" Matthew asked.

"What?" Jenna said.

"Did that before, when I…planned to run with Eli." He looked at his son. "I thought I could keep him safe. I thought…"

"You can still keep him safe," Matthew said. "Give us something to shut down the cartel."

"This is your chance to be a hero for your son," Jenna added.

Gary nodded, a tear trailing down the side of his face. "There's a flash drive in his bear. It has everything, recordings, accounts."

Matthew glanced at the bear Eli clutched in his hand.

Gary's eyes misted over, and he looked at Eli. "I'm so sorry. I love you, tiger."

Eli pressed his cheek against Jenna's shoulder.

"Eli, your papa has an ow-ee," Jenna said. "He needs a kiss."

"Ow-ee." Eli touched his head where he'd bumped into the window frame at the Millers' farm.

"Can you give him a kiss to make it better?" Jenna encouraged.

Eli whipped his head around and looked at his dad. Jenna put Eli down. He leaned forward and kissed Gary on the nose.

"What a good boy," Jenna said.

Eli turned to Jenna and hugged her.

"Feels…much better," Gary said, before his eyelids fluttered closed.

THIRTEEN

"They were after Eli to control his father?" Patrice asked, as they sat in a conference room at the FBI field office.

"Looks that way." Jenna offered Eli a sippy cup with water, but he was more interested in playing with his wooden trains.

Jenna, Eli and Patrice had been taken to a field office to make their statements. Matthew rode with them, but said little.

Unfortunately Gary hadn't survived.

"And Anthony… I still can't believe he got early release and found you," Patrice said.

"He'd hired someone to break into my attorney's office and found my address, a PO box in Cedar River. From there, he hired a private detective, who eventually tracked me down. Anthony had him go through my apartment." Jenna shuddered. "I remembered thinking things were out of place, but figured it was posttrauma paranoia."

"You thought it was over with Anthony."

"The PI kept me under surveillance and became familiar with my routine. Somehow he got access to my messenger bag and put a tracking device inside so he'd always know where I was." She hesitated. "So Anthony would always know."

"How long had this been going on?"

"A couple of months."

"What was Anthony waiting for?"

"He only got out a few weeks ago. My guess is he enjoyed the hunt, planning what he'd do to me in retaliation for sending him to jail. We had all kinds of criminals tracking us. Just when we thought we were safe at the Lazy Shade Resort, Anthony sent thugs to kidnap me. When that didn't work, and knowing that I was wanted for kidnapping Eli, Anthony contacted Billings. They probably had a great time planning my demise."

"Someone should have notified you that Anthony had been released."

"For all I know there's a letter waiting for me in the PO box, but I only check it periodically. I honestly thought he was done with me."

"The man was a bully."

"I'm sorry you got caught up in all this. I never should have called you."

"Yes you should have. As I said many times

when you stayed with me, we can't face our challenges alone, nor should we have to."

"But the Guardians... Have I put them in jeopardy?"

"No. Your friend Matthew gave me his word he wouldn't expose our network. Who knows, maybe someday the FBI will need our help."

"I love your attitude."

Patrice glanced at Eli. "And you love that little boy, don't you?"

Jenna nodded, smiling at Eli as he made a choo-choo sound.

"And Agent Weller?" Patrice said.

"He loves Eli too."

"I meant, how do you feel about Agent Weller?"

Jenna snapped her gaze to Patrice. "I know, these feelings are inappropriate," Jenna said.

"I didn't say that."

"You were about to. I get it. Only—" She hesitated. "He's the first man who has ever made me feel safe."

"That says a lot, considering what you've been through this past week."

"I guess."

"What is it?"

"I'm not sure he feels the same way." *Even though he's held me, comforted me...kissed me.*

"Well, the way he asked me to help him find

you sounded more like the plea of a man in love than that of an FBI agent."

The door opened, and Matthew nodded at Patrice. "They're ready to take your statement."

Patrice patted Jenna on the hand and left.

"How's the little guy doin'?" Matthew asked, sitting at the conference table beside Jenna.

"He's great."

Silence permeated the room. There was so much to say, but how to say it?

"What will happen to Eli?" she asked.

"Marcus is on the way."

Jenna nodded, fighting back the grief at having to say goodbye to the adorable child.

Would she have to say goodbye to Matthew as well?

"What a crazy week," she said. "Is your case solid against the cartel?"

"Yes, ma'am. Everything's on the flash drive, just as Gary said."

"Why didn't he turn it over to the authorities earlier?"

"He wanted to avoid making enemies with the cartel. He hoped to control the situation and stop having to move money around for them. The cartel hired Billings to keep an eye on Gary. I suspect Billings has been corrupt since his days as a border patrol agent."

"Yikes."

"Gary wanted out. The cartel refused. Gary

figured he'd use blackmail, like he did with corporations, but the cartel decided to go after his family. At the end of the day you'd do anything to protect your family."

"So true."

Another awkward silence.

"I'm glad your ex-husband will never hurt you again," Matthew said.

"Thank you."

He glanced at her with regret in his eyes. "I'm sorry."

"For what?"

"For failing you, for not being there when you needed me most."

"But you *were* there for us at the barn, and you saved us so many times before that."

"Jenna—"

"Hear me out, Matt. Facing off against Billings and my ex-husband on my own wouldn't have been my first choice, yet it gave me such strength, strength I never knew I had."

He shook his head and glanced down at the floor. "You never should have left me behind."

"You mean at the hospital?"

"I understand why you did it—"

"Because you were bleeding to death."

"Because you no longer felt safe around me."

"Whoa, you're going to have to explain that one."

Eli ran up to her with a blue train. "Choo-choo!"

Without taking her eyes off Matt, she joined

Eli on the floor and started playing trains with him. "Matt?" she prompted.

"The guy in the rental cabin—you saw me almost beat him to death."

"Because he tried to kill me," she stated. "Go on."

"You saw what I'm capable of."

"Didn't you see what I am capable of? Anthony's bloody nose and bloody shoulder? That was me. I may not have fired the bullet that killed him, but I shot him to protect Eli. That's what we do for the people we love."

Whoops.

He looked up, pinning her with intense blue eyes.

"I love Eli, don't you?" she fumbled, correcting herself.

His gaze drifted to the little boy, then back to Jenna.

He was about to say something when someone tapped on the door and it cracked open. A man introduced himself to Jenna as Supervisory Special Agent Steve Pragge. "Glad to see you and the little guy are okay, ma'am."

"Thanks to Agent Weller," she said, to drive her point home.

Matt was no longer looking at her.

"He kept us safe," Jenna added, concerned about how she'd craft her argument to Matt once they were alone. She couldn't make him admit he was in love with her, nor should she have to.

"Bubba," Eli said.

Jenna grabbed a replacement white bear and handed it to him. He frowned and turned back to his train.

"Weller certainly went off book on this one," his boss said. "Defied a direct order to drop you off and go back to his post."

She wondered if Matt's job would be in jeopardy because he'd decided to protect her and Eli.

"But his instincts to stay with you helped us build this case," Pragge said. "That's what makes a good agent, putting the job first."

Ah, the job—the perfect excuse for Matt to distance himself from Jenna and deny his feelings. He'd held her in his arms and made her feel safe, even loved. He'd probably argue those were the actions of a man just doing his job. Hogwash.

"The flash drive outlines everything," Pragge continued. "It's an indisputable link from the cartel to the money-laundering scheme to Billings. We've got Billings on video killing Chloe McFadden. He'd wiped the building's feed, but apparently Gary had set up his own cameras to keep track of things at the foundation. Billings is turning state's evidence in exchange for negotiating his prison location. As a cop, he wouldn't survive long in the general population."

"Well, I can make myself available to testify if you need me," Jenna offered.

"I appreciate that." Glancing at his phone, Pragge said, "I've gotta take this."

He left Jenna and Matthew alone. Tension stretched between them.

"You sure you'd be up to testifying if they need you to?" Matthew asked.

"Matthew, I'm a strong woman and I'll do what's right by my friend."

"I know you're strong, Jenna. I'm just doing my job by—"

"Really, Matt?" She stood and squared off with him. "So your question has nothing to do with your feelings for me?"

He glanced down at the industrial carpeting. "I'm sorry if I led you to believe—"

"Stop, okay? Stop using your job as an excuse so you won't have to admit the truth." She didn't know where this bold woman had come from, but she liked her, and it felt amazing to articulate her truth in such a raw and vulnerable way. "Hey, look at me."

When he did, she thought she might lose her nerve. His expression was guarded, his eyes shuttered.

"You can say the danger of the past week drove us into each other's arms, but it's more than that and you know it," she said. "God knows it."

"There's no room in my life for a relationship."

"Why not?"

"If Sarah's death proved anything, it's that I'm not good husband material."

"Sarah made a choice. She chose to drive recklessly. Now it's your turn to choose. Are you going to embrace love or run away from it?" Jenna picked up Eli. "We're going to thc fountain for a drink."

She was unable to stand there one minute longer arguing with him about what was so obvious to Jenna. As she reached the door, she hesitated. Maybe if he wouldn't listen to her, he'd listen to God.

"Isn't there a quote in the Bible about truth, about it setting you free?" she said. "I think you should find that scripture."

She left the conference room and approached the fountain, knowing it would entertain Eli to slurp up the cold water. Besides, she needed to get away from Matt and his denial. For the first time in her life, she knew the truth in her heart—Matt loved her just as she loved him.

"Hey, Jenna." Marcus approached her, alongside special agent Pragge.

She took a deep breath and forced a smile.

The time had come for her to say goodbye, not only to the man she loved, but to the little boy she loved as well.

"Hi, Marcus," she said with forced charm. "I'm so glad you're okay."

"You as well." He reached out for Eli, but the little guy clung to Jenna.

"Eli, you remember Marcus?" she encouraged.

Be strong, Jenna, stronger than you've ever been in your life.

"Bubba." Eli rubbed his eyes.

"I think he forgot something." Matt joined them in the hallway, carrying the white bear. He offered it to Eli, but the child knew it wasn't his real bear, which had been confiscated for evidence.

Eli started to whimper.

"It's okay, buddy," she said, stroking his back.

"Or this?" Matt offered the Binky.

She took it and placed it in Eli's mouth. Eli sucked and leaned his head against her shoulder.

"You're gonna have fun with your cousin Marcus, little one," she said.

Please, God, help me do this without upsetting Eli.

She gripped him under the arms and peeled him off her, pain arcing through her chest. She smiled and kissed his cheek. "Love you, buddy."

As she handed him to Marcus, Eli whimpered against his pacifier.

"He likes multigrain bars and apples for breakfast. Scrambled eggs would be good too. But no more bottles at mealtime."

Marcus took the whimpering child.

Jenna turned and walked away. "Big boys use sippy cups."

She purposefully walked down the hall to the ladies' bathroom, rushed up to the mirror and took a deep breath. The tears broke free, and for the first time she was okay with that, accepting herself and even forgiving herself for crying. She finally understood that crying was not a sign of weakness, as Anthony had claimed, but a cleansing of emotions.

And she had plenty of those.

It took a good month before things settled down and Matt could return to Cedar River. He wanted to meet with Kyle, who'd temporarily taken over as police chief. Matt owed his friend an explanation and an apology.

"I wish I could have told you what was going on," Matt said to Kyle as they sat in the Bean & Brew Coffee Shop on Main Street. "Sorry about that."

"Hey, I get it. You were doing your job." Kyle sipped his coffee. "Where are you off to next? Another undercover assignment?"

"They've offered me a Supervisory Special Agent position."

"That's great news. Congratulations." He reached out to shake Matt's hand.

Matt stared into his mug.

"That is great news, right?" Kyle withdrew his hand.

A month ago a promotion like this would have been Matt's ultimate goal, his brass ring. Today, well, today he felt like there had to be more to life than a demanding, all-consuming career.

Perhaps a life with a special, loving woman and even children?

The memory of Jenna's smile flashed across his mind—her smile and Eli's giggle.

"Have you seen her yet?" Kyle asked.

Matt snapped his attention to his friend. "Who?"

"Jenna North."

"No, why would I… Wait, you mean she came back here?"

Kyle nodded.

Matt wouldn't know her whereabouts because he'd intentionally avoided anything relating to Jenna, wanting to put it all behind him. He'd even tried to avoid thinking about her, although on most days he'd failed miserably.

"The little boy is with her," Kyle added.

"Eli? I thought Marcus was his guardian."

"Marcus came into the station and introduced himself. Nice guy. I got the feeling he can't be a full-time parent because of his business, so he and Jenna have an arrangement."

"What kind of arrangement?" Matt growled.

Kyle chuckled. "It's not like that. They're both

committed to doing what's best for the boy. Marcus bought property half an hour outside of town, and I'm guessing he bought the bungalow Jenna's living in as well. It's down the block from me, Garth and Willie."

"She moved into a cop neighborhood?"

"Yep. The town has really rallied around her to offer support."

"That's great."

"It's one of the reasons I love this place. You kinda liked it too when you lived here, didn't you?"

"I did. I liked it a lot." It was the one time Matt had felt like he truly belonged and was accepted for who he was, not for his level of performance.

"So, you're here, she's here…why not stop by?"

"It's complicated."

"No, it really isn't. You care about her, she cares about you—"

"Why do you say that? Did she say something?"

"No, and I won't pass her a note from you in class either. Come on, Matt, it's obvious."

"What's obvious is she needs a devoted man with integrity who makes her feel safe and is good with kids."

"Not that you are even close to fitting that description," Kyle teased. "My turn to share scripture. John chapter eight verse thirty-two."

"You're the second person to mention that particular scripture to me."

"Yeah, well." Kyle leaned back in his chair. "It's a good one, my friend."

There was nothing more beautiful than a sleeping child, Jenna thought as she stood over Eli's crib. He made a sweet little squeaking sound as he exhaled, clutching his new Bubba tighter.

She was glad he'd finally embraced the new stuffed animal with as much vigor as he'd had for the original.

Eli somehow had been able to leave the past behind and move on. He didn't cry too much for his parents, but then, she and friends in town had kept him fairly occupied.

Friends. She thought she'd only had one good friend, Chloe, but had been proven wrong this past month. Ladies from Bible study stopped by to help her unpack and offer parenting advice. The police officers in the neighborhood came by to make sure she felt safe and to share their cell numbers. One of the officer's wives brought dinner and, knowing her husband was working the 3 to 11 p.m. shift, Jenna invited her to stay. The other officer's wife took Eli for a few hours twice a week for a playdate with her toddler. The third police officer in the neighborhood was Kyle Armstrong, who wasn't married and was Matthew's friend.

Matthew.

She shook off the memory of a lovely kiss and sneaked quietly out of Eli's room. Shutting the door, she scanned the living room littered with toy trucks, trains and even a small playpen filled with plastic balls. The people of Cedar River had been incredibly supportive and didn't blame Jenna for the community center being shut down due to the investigation.

Jenna had been out of a job for only a few days when Marcus showed up with Eli. Marcus pleaded with Jenna to help him raise the little boy. She thought she was dreaming at first. She could hardly believe Eli was really there, reaching for her.

Marcus said parenting seemed to come so naturally to Jenna and she'd proven she could protect the child. They drew up guardianship paperwork, and Marcus encouraged Jenna to consider officially adopting Eli.

She didn't hesitate to contact an attorney and get things started.

Marcus offered financial support for Jenna and the child, but then they got word that Gary's will left everything to Eli in the form of a trust, and Jenna was the trustee. He'd revised the will only days before his own death. They'd have to wait for the case to be solved first, to make sure none of the money he'd left Eli was the result of criminal activity, but so far it looked like a separate account with legitimate money would be available, according to Agent Pragge.

She'd been in touch with either him or Agent Barnes, but not Matthew. It was as if he had no interest in what happened to Jenna.

Shaking off the thought, she kneeled on the living room floor and picked up blocks. Although exhausted from taking care of Eli, loving this little boy also energized her.

There was a soft tap at the front door. Marcus had insisted she get a video surveillance app on her phone that allowed her to see who was there.

Pulling the phone out of her pocket, she clicked on the app. And gasped at the sight of Matthew's handsome face filling her screen.

She sprung up from the floor and automatically ran her hands through her hair, wishing she'd put on blush or mascara today, but there hadn't been time.

"He's probably here on business," she muttered. That had to be it.

She took a deep breath. Opened the door.

He offered her a bouquet of daisies.

"Wow, thank you, Matthew. They're beautiful."

"I brought some stuff for the little guy too." He nodded at a shopping bag beside him on the porch.

"Come in," she said. "Is this about the case?"

"No, everything's good there."

Which meant…

Excitement fluttered in her belly. She led him toward the kitchen in the back of the house.

"Nice house," he said.

"Thanks. It's perfect for Eli and me. No stairs for me to worry about, and nice soft carpeting in case he takes a tumble." She pulled a water pitcher down from the cabinet to use as a vase.

"Looks like they've done some good updates. I noticed new windows. That should keep the house warm in the winter."

"It has so far." She filled the pitcher with water.

"I suppose you've got an energy efficient furnace?"

"Is that why you're here? To discuss my heating and cooling system?" she teased, turning to him.

"Sorry, no. I just…" He sighed and held her gaze. "John chapter eight verse thirty-two."

"What?"

"'Then you will know the truth, and the truth will set you free.' That's the scripture you were referring to."

"Oh."

"You're right, it did set me free once I admitted it to myself."

"Admitted…?"

"I always thought the job was my first priority, that I wouldn't give it up for anyone. The truth is, I hadn't found the woman I wanted to give it up for."

She was speechless at first, and then said, "Wait, you're leaving the FBI?"

"Maybe, I don't know. It depends."

"On what?"

"On you."

"I don't understand."

"Sure you do." He smiled. "I've missed you."

Her heart burst, and she went into his arms. As they clung to each other in the small kitchen, she thanked God for showing Matthew the way back to her.

Jenna leaned back and looked up into his smiling face. "What does this all mean, Matt?"

"It means I love you and we'll figure out the rest as we go."

"I have never felt so blessed in my life," she said.

He brushed a soft kiss against her lips. "Amen to that."

* * * * *

Dear Reader,

Our past experiences, including traumatic events, shape who we are as human beings. At the time we are going through challenging situations, we might lose hope and wonder if we'll survive. Yet sometimes we come out of these situations as stronger people with new skills and insights into our lives and the lives of others.

Having survived an abusive marriage and the loss of her unborn child, Jenna North created a new identity and started a life away from the pain of her past. But when her friend's child is suddenly in danger, Jenna must draw strength from her own personal tragedy and protect little Eli. Throughout the course of the story, Jenna realizes that running doesn't put the pain behind her, and she can gain strength from facing the fear.

FBI agent Matt Weller is the ideal man to help Jenna find her confidence and strength as he protects her from criminals threatening her life and that of little Eli. Matt's faith has helped him cope with personal tragedy, and his recovery from the pain is a good example for Jenna to witness.

As they rely on each other to protect a toddler from harm, Jenna and Matt exemplify teamwork and the blessing that we need not handle personal challenges alone. I'm ever so grateful for my family, friends and God, who help me along the way.

Peace,
Hope White